Her Guardian Wolf

Black Hills Wolves 48

By
Jax Garren

Copyright © 2016 by Jax Garren
ISBN: 978-1-68361-030-4
Cover art by Fiona Jayde

Published by Decadent Publishing Company, LLC
Look for us online at:
www.decadentpublishing.com

~A Note from Jax~

Dear Reader,

Thanks for joining me in the Black Hills!

When I was a kid, I was fascinated by the Black Hills goldsmiths who blend metals to create multi-colored gold and craft jewelry from it. When I decided to write a story in the Black Hills Wolves series, I knew Elle, my heroine would be a metalsmith who crafts her own line of amazing jewelry—though with a modern edge. I paired her with Caleb, a motorcycle-riding fireman who can't wait to claim her as his mate, and then mixed in the danger of another wolf, Elle's creepy ex-boyfriend, who isn't willing to let her go.

I write paranormal romance and romantic urban fantasy that champions everyday people. Elle and Caleb practically wrote themselves, two people—er, a person and a werewolf!—with dreams and baggage trying to find family in a complicated world. I hope you have as much fun reading their journey as I did writing it! I'd love to hear your thoughts at jennifercgarren@gmail.com or on Facebook at JaxGarren or Twitter at @JCGarren.

Cheers!
Jax

Dedication

To the Digital Darlings. Thanks for the cheese. Thanks for the motivation. Most of all, thanks for the friendship.

Chapter One

Elle Montgomery kept the security chain attached as she stared at her ex through the cracked door. Despite the fear curling through her belly, she forced her voice to remain calm. "I told you. We're done. Go away before I call the police."

Phillip whined a noise more animal than human, his glower as frighteningly desperate as the day she'd walked out of his home with one suitcase and what remained of her pride. "You can't, Elle. You're my mate. We're forever."

She pounded her head against the doorjamb two times. Phillip's use of "mate" didn't sound like Australian for "friend." He meant it like an animal finding a sexual partner. She wasn't an animal, but there were times she wondered about him. In the beginning, he'd been so sweet, but then they'd moved in together and things changed. *He* changed. "We broke up. It happens. I appreciate our time together, but you need to move on. If you'll excuse me, I'm in the middle of work." On the shelf of a balcony in her new apartment, her blowtorch and other tools waited for her return. The half-complete necklace on the workbench was her first project for a big-name star, a make-or-break career move that needed to be perfect. She didn't have time to deal with Phillip and his mood swings.

"I got you the commission, and now you won't talk to me?"

The advantages Phillip's money and connections were extraordinary. The disadvantages of his temper—they were why she kept the chain attached. He'd never hurt her, not badly anyway. Not yet. She'd left before she found out exactly how angry he could get. "You helped me get the meeting, but the quality of my work got me the commission, and my arm is still bruised from your grip. Go away."

The whine turned to a full-on growl, the kind an enraged dog made. She backed up a step as the hair on her neck stood up. Suddenly the chain didn't feel like enough. His brown eyes turned amber, almost glowing in the shadows of her apartment front stoop—surely a trick of the light. He slammed his palm into the door. The chain stretched taut, the wood around the metal catch cracking with the force. Her heart stopped at the noise. But the chain held. For now. "There is no moving on for me, mate. We're forever."

Enough was enough. "I'm calling the police." She shoved the door shut, her heart pounding.

He shoved back. The chain snapped and the door bounced open, slamming into her. She reeled back, cheek and shoulder stinging from the impact. Fear, thick and oppressive, turned her skin to ice. Phillip entered her apartment and shut the door behind him. His gaze bored into her, trapping her in its dangerous intensity as he stalked forward.

She backed up. Her steps were heavy and awkward in her work boots while he slunk forward with steady menace in thousand dollar shoes. "I put up with your little cry for independence, mate, but this has gone on too long." She backed into a wall. He slammed an arm above her head and leaned in until she could feel his breath against her forehead. "We're forever. Fate decreed it. You can't escape fate."

"There is no fate." She rammed her knee up. He leaped back, so fast—too fast—but it gave her room. She dodged past him and into the bedroom. If she could reach the balcony, she'd have options—swing over it, yell for help, hell, blast him with her fucking torch—anything but trapped in an apartment with a man whose sanity was degrading at record speed.

Oshun, the Abyssinian cat she'd adopted last week, hissed and spit, their angry terror mutual. "Come!" she yelled, and for once the stupid cat followed orders and ran with her for the sliding door. She got her fingers on the handle.

Phillip's hand clapped onto her shoulder from behind. "You will stay!"

"No! Fate doesn't decide this. We do. We decide for ourselves. And I decided no!"

Metal clicked around her wrist, and his arm curved around her stomach, squeezing the air from her lungs as he hauled her backward.

"Bastard! Let me go!" Fear and anger brought tears to her eyes as she kicked and fought. His strength caged her against him. He'd always been so damn strong. He'd never lost it like this, either.

Another click, and she was handcuffed to the bed.

Phillip backed up, finally granting her space to breathe. "We're different, mate, you and I. Fated." He shed his jacket and shoes and unbuttoned the first few buttons of his shirt. "And you're going to see why."

She grabbed a picture of her mother off the bedside table, ready to hit him with the metal frame when he came near.

He didn't approach. He looked up at the ceiling, and his face seemed to change, elongating. It had to be a trick of light or maybe she'd hit her head harder than she realized.

Then his body shifted, too. His arms stretched and narrowed as he leaned down to all fours. The crack of realigning bones made her twitch in empathetic pain. How did he keep from screaming? His clothes fell off, shedding like snake skin as fur sprouted.

She gasped, trying to reconcile what she saw with reality. Phillip had transformed into a wolf.

He padded forward on four legs. Long canines shone in the sunlight. His amber eyes were wild in their inhuman gaze. He butted his head against her, wiry fur scraping her jaw and neck.

Terror blanked her thoughts. She screamed. Screamed again. Launched backward until the handcuff caught, and she curled into the corner sobbing.

The fur disappeared, turning back to human skin. "Sh, sh, sh. Baby, it's okay. I'd never hurt you. It's okay."

"You're a...you're a...."

"A werewolf. Yes. And you're my mate." His fingers touched her skin in motions meant to soothe, but each cold touch made her want to scream again. He was a monster, and he thought he owned her.

"Go away. Oh, go away. Please go away."

His forehead pressed against her temple as his fingers dug into her possessively. Each touch brought more tears. To her surprise, he pulled back. "I understand this is hard to take. But you needed to know why you can't leave me." His eyes stayed hard as he shook his head, like a teacher to an errant pupil. "I only get one mate, Elle. I'll be true to you forever. I'll protect you and love you. Nobody else will ever have you. But you can't leave. You can never leave me. All you have to do is stay and be a good woman to me, and I'll make your life perfect."

Crazy talk. He was a monster, and he was fucking insane. This sweetness scared her more than the violence of earlier. He believed what he said. He thought of her as his possession, his pet to comfort and cosset as long as she heeled on command.

He backed up farther, sighing as he righted his clothes, all askew from the transformation. His suit back in perfect place, he stood. "I understand this is hard for you. I'm going to give you a few minutes. I'll get us coffee. I know exactly how you want it. See, I want to please you. I *need* to. The drive is consuming. Make it easy for me to make you happy." He patted a fist to his chest where his heart should be. He didn't have a heart, just the instincts of an animal. "I will give you everything you want. But you can't leave again, Elle. You and I are forever." He went to the door and searched the nearby tables, the places where he would keep his keys and other morning "launch" items in his systematic way. More than one argument between them had sparked over her more

5

lackadaisical style. Mouth pinched in irritation, he turned to her. "Where are they?"

Her keys were in the kitchen and nowhere near the front door, thank God. She narrowed her eyes. "Like I'm telling you shit."

His back stiffened, but he kept his cool as he clicked every lock on the front door. "You will learn better. Take a few minutes to calm down. When I return with your coffee, you're coming home with me."

Fear brought her knees to her chest, and she clutched them. He could force her to leave with him. With his strength, he could force her to do anything. Plus he was wealthy and white from a family with an old name. She was black and barely making ends meet as an artisan. Not only could he physically carry her away, he likely thought he could get away with it. Hell, maybe he could.

He stooped beside her. She tried to dodge him, but he got a hand firmly on her chin. His touch seemed familiar yet utterly changed by his behavior. Months they'd been together. How had she not seen him for what he really was? He kissed her head, his lips lingering too long on her hair. She started to shake.

"It's going to be okay, Elle. You're mine. I'll make you happy." He headed for the balcony. She lost sight of him for a minute, and then he launched himself over the edge of her third-story place, easy and light as an animal.

Because he *was* an animal. She'd dated a fucking werewolf and not realized it. She rattled the handcuff, but nothing budged. She looked toward the balcony. She'd left her phone there with her crafting supplies, out of reach.

Oshun prowled by and head butted her. She rubbed the cat's neck, trying to take comfort from the soft fur, so unlike the stiff canine bristles Phillip had shoved against her. She needed a plan. She needed to think. What would happen when Phillip came back?

The cat's enormous ears perked up, and Elle turned toward the balcony, alarmed. *Shit*. Could Phillip be back already? There was no way he'd gotten coffee. Maybe the crazy asshole went nowhere then hopped back up the freaking balcony. Oshun's head weaved back and forth again before she dashed under the bed, freaked out, but no sounds came crashing into the apartment and no Phillip appeared. Elle stretched as far as she could toward the balcony but couldn't see anything. No sounds came. Nothing....

No. Not nothing. Smoke. The scent of burning wood hit her nose—wood smoke and melting plastic.

Her welding equipment.

A fire must've started on her balcony. She needed to contain it. Thousands of dollars in precious metal, all her equipment, her project—the one that would make her career—were out there, soon to melt into useless pools. Everything else she owned could burn to ash and she wouldn't care, but the safe full of gold, copper, silver, and precious stones, the pieces of her latest design, she needed those. She yanked so hard on the handcuff, the metal bit into her hand.

Had Phillip started a fire? For what purpose? Other than he'd turned psychotic.

She stretched up to her bedside table and grabbed a bobby pin. She had no idea how to pick a lock, but figuring it out right now would be perfect timing.

After she spent minutes uselessly jamming at the lock, the fire climbed the doorframe into her room. Smoke blew in, thick against the ceiling. She coughed. The heat blazed, and sweat streamed down the back of her neck. If the fire didn't get under control, it wasn't merely her life's work in danger, it was the whole complex—with her locked in it.

Oshun howled, her meow strained and pathetic. How much smoke could a cat take before she died from asphyxiation? Elle's heart lurched as she thought of her beautiful girl dying under the bed.

Giving up on the lock, Elle stood as tall as she could, stooping because of the fucking handcuff. Stretching until her shoulder hurt with strain, she managed to shove open a window. A tree branch nearly jutted inside. Oshun could escape without running through the fire on the balcony.

Tears streamed down Elle's face as she reached under the bed. "Oshun! Go, you stupid cat! Get out!" The handcuff around her wrist seared her skin, heating up with the rising flames, but she pulled against it anyway, desperate for the last few inches she needed to reach the kitty. She may be trapped, but she could save Oshun before the fire creeping across her ceiling killed them both.

If the damn cat would listen to her.

Smoke with its acrid stench hung heavy in the air, choking her. She squeezed her eyes against the sting, punched the carpet, and screamed as rage consumed her. She was going to die handcuffed to an iron bed. Hatred burned through her veins, hot as the out-of-control fire.

"Oshun! Get your furry ass over here!" The damn

cat hissed at her. Sirens rang. Fire trucks? Hope made her renew her efforts.

Footsteps pounded. Firemen? Somebody? She screamed as loudly as she could and sucked in lungs full of toxic air. Sputtering and coughing she beat her fist against the wall to keep up the noise. Screamed again as soon as she could.

Someone banged on her door. She kicked the floor, rattled the handcuff, whatever sound she could make. If she couldn't get them into the bedroom....

The front door crashed open. She renewed her noise efforts, managed another scream. Her eyes burned from smoke, but still she watched her bedroom door, determined to live.

Two men in yellow entered.

Eyes the blue of dawn sky widened at the sight of her. She yanked her cuff. In a blur of motion he came to her side and his ax slammed into the chain, freeing her.

She was going to live.

She dove under the bed for Oshun. Her hand got around the cat's back legs just before someone yanked her out, dragging Oshun with her.

Oshun struggled and clawed at the floor. The fireman's eyes widened, and he grabbed the cat in big hands made bigger with gloves. He passed the animal off to the second fireman and pointed at the door. "Go. I got her."

Elle didn't wait. She dashed through a line of flame, glad for her leather work boots as heat rolled over her shoulders and made her eyes water. She shoved her hands into her welding gloves, shoved her latest work into the metal safe, slammed the lid, and picked up the box containing her livelihood.

Her hips were grabbed from behind, and the fireman pulled her to him then up and over his shoulder. She held tight to the box as he ran, his arms firm around her. As the cooler air of the stairwell hit her skin, she started to shiver. Then she started to cry.

She wasn't going to die.

Adam Hunt set the crazy woman on her feet next to the ambulance and ripped his mask off, ready to read her the riot act. Who the hell ran *toward* the fire's center? Her knees gave out, and she started to collapse. He caught her.

Over the alarming scents of smoke and salty sweat, the richness of vanilla and earthiness stalled his anger and, unaccountably considering the situation, turned him on. He didn't want to yell anymore; he wanted to hold her and protect her from the threats of the world. Confused, he looked into her dark eyes, and vertigo hit him stronger than at the apex of the highest roller coaster.

Mate.

The roller coaster dove, and his stomach lurched in fear and exhilaration. He'd just hauled his mate, the one woman fate had selected for him, out of a burning apartment complex. He held her tighter, a reflex he couldn't suppress. *My mate.* And to think he'd been pissed when a call came in five minutes from his clock out, delaying the time until he could hit O'Shaughnessey's and feel the sweet burn and fog of alcohol. The desire for drunken oblivion remained, same as it had ever since he'd left his pack, banished and shamed. But her presence overwhelmed it, muffling its call into an ignorable buzz.

He carried her to a bench. Her hands clung to his collar as her teeth chattered in shock. He pulled her into his lap. The bulky Nomex and Kevlar of his jacket impeded his ability to embrace her. She didn't need a tirade. She needed comfort, and he wanted to give it to her. "You're okay," he finally managed. "I got you. You're okay."

Her hands shook as she pushed out of his lap and onto the bench. His wolf drove him to hang onto the fragile human who ran toward fire, but his human logic knew he didn't normally sit fire victims on his lap. She would think it strange, so he let her slide away. She clutched a lockbox in one gloved hand. The other still held onto his jacket. "Thank you," she muttered then said again, louder, "Thank you." She looked around. "Where's Oshun?"

He pursed his lips. Had smoke inhalation confused her? "We're in Denver. The ocean's pretty far away."

Her eyes finally focused on his, and she gave a half-hearted laugh. "My cat. Oshun's an African goddess." Big eyes, deepest brown, turned worried. The whites shone bright and tearful against smooth, dark skin. She looked like an African goddess herself, brave and beautiful.

Awkward in his fire gloves, he released a spiral curl stuck to her tear- and sweat-damp cheek. He shouldn't nuzzle her, despite his wolf insisting it was a terrific idea. Would she think him weird if he got a tissue and dried her face?

"She's safe, right?" the woman insisted.

His mate needed something. Her first request. That, he could do. "Your cat's safe. Tim has her." He searched the chaos of the street in front of her apartment. Three trucks had arrived—more than necessary, but for once he was happy for the extra expense. A typical crowd had gathered to gawk, intermingled with tearful residents watching in hopeless fear as their lives went up in fire and smoke.

They'd gotten to the fire early and could save most of the building. His mate's room, though, the likely source of the fire, would be mostly lost. How could he best help her recover?

Fear tightened his chest as he thought of what would've happened if they hadn't come so soon. Best not to dwell. Eventually he spotted Tim, his partner on the inside, trying to keep hold of a howling animal.

His mate owned a...cat. She'd said so; he'd even held the thing for a couple seconds, but the sight of the animal now made it register. That was not going to go well.

His partner's face relaxed in relief, and he headed their way. The man loved animals, but angry cats drove everyone nuts.

"There's your little goddess." Adam pointed the cat out, and his mate relaxed.

She started to get up, but her legs trembled so much she sat immediately, eyes cast down in embarrassment.

He put a steadying hand on her shoulder. "You've had a shock. Give your legs a few minutes."

"I'm not usually so shaky." She squeezed the handle of the safe like an awkward teddy bear.

"What's in the box?" *That you risked your life for?*

"My work. I'm a jewelry maker." She pursed her

lips then released. "I guess you think I'm crazy for going toward the fire."

Yeah. He really did. But she was safe now, and he'd seen people go back into burning buildings for all sorts of stupid reasons.

Her mouth twisted up as if she contemplated something—her mouth was so expressive; he loved it—then she opened the case enough for him to peek in, displaying ingots of gold, copper, and other precious metals. Thousands of dollars worth.

"Holy shit." *Oops*. "Excuse my language."

With a firmer laugh, she snapped the case shut. "I'm working on a commission. I can't afford to buy the materials twice, but once this is done, I'm on my way to a real income." She patted the box with her still-gloved hands. "Getting new equipment will be a PITA, but what's in here is my life's work—success or failure in a one-foot cube." She set the case between her feet and pushed up to standing as Tim arrived and handed her Oshun.

The terrified pet didn't seem much happier, even with her owner. Stupid cat. He couldn't imagine a circumstance in which he'd try to escape being pressed against her body. The animal hissed at him, spitting and swiping like it would challenge a mature werewolf.

He cocked his head to the side and made eye contact, staring it down. The thing backed up, crouching in his mate's arms as it continued to hiss.

"Oshun! Be nice. He saved our lives." She sighed. "No thanks to you, you stupid cat. Cats don't listen." She said the last bit like a compliment then looked back at him, somehow keeping the bristling animal in her arms. "What's your name? I'm Elle Montgomery."

A stupid smile lifted his cheeks. His mate possessed a beautiful name. He stuck a hand out, and she shook it, her thick canvas glove enfolded easily in his leather and Nomex one. "Adam Hunt." They stood awkwardly for a moment. He wanted to say more but didn't know where to start. *Hi! I'm a werewolf and you're my mate!* was unlikely to go over well. "Stay here," he finally said. "I want to find you afterward." The words exited his mouth, and he wanted to bite them back. *That wasn't at all dickish, Hunt. Why don't you try bossing her around more. Women love it.*

Instead of getting upset, she shrank a little, her shoulder coming close to his as if she wanted comfort but refused to ask for it. He knew the feeling. But there seemed to be more to her unease than the fire. The fear in her eyes as her gaze darted around the growing crush of bodies set off alarms in his head. His mate should never be afraid, and right now fear rode her hard. Fear of what?

He frowned. When he'd entered the room, she'd been handcuffed to the bed. He'd assumed she had been playing some kinky game—whatever floated her boat right? Although now the thought of some other man....

Push it back, Hunt. Don't think about it. She wore work boots, though. And the position of the cuff didn't really make sense, low to the ground putting her face down onto the bed with one arm stretched at a funny angle. Not that he couldn't figure out something interesting to do with his mate in any position.

This time he did bite his tongue, focusing on the pain to bring him back to the here and now.

Envisioning naked, handcuffed Elle was not only inappropriate at the moment, it wasn't going to help him help her. He smelled the wind blowing across her to him. She smelled human, which meant she wouldn't feel the same instant desire he did. He needed to entice her into a relationship.

He liked a challenge.

He shook his head, trying to back off from visions of a lifetime of hot sex and steady companionship and focus on immediate needs. His mate had been handcuffed to a bed in work boots, and her welding equipment was likely what caused the fire.

The clues added up to somebody did this on purpose.

To his mate.

He sucked back a growl and scanned the crowd again, this time looking for somebody with a death wish. "Tim," he said, slapping his partner's shoulder with the back of his hand. "Think they've got the situation covered?" The blaze was contained and firemen still crawled all over the place. At this point, more people got in the way and made things harder.

Tim tsked in irritation. "We got enough men to stop a block of fires. After all the crap going on across the country with cops, Chief wants to make sure the ghetto feels loved by the fire department."

Elle lifted her brow, expression pointed. "The ghetto, huh?"

Tim's eyes went wide, hands up as his mistake caught up with him. Adam blew out a breath as he realized he might not have noticed the insult yesterday. Now, though, standing next to his mate, trying to see the world through her eyes, it sounded damn racist.

"Sorry, ma'am," Tim said. "I mean to say, there's a shit ton of people. You're covered. Hunt, if you want to take off. I know it's past your shift." His partner dashed off in a hustle, getting away from Elle and the dangerous arch of her eyebrows.

Adam pulled his gloves off and reached for her arm. He touched her elbow, a cotton shirt still separating them. Even through the fabric, the touch hummed and sparked. It excited him yet calmed him. The noise in his head, the angry desires driving him to go to the bar because he couldn't go back home to his pack in the Black Hills, the bleak day to day that needed alcohol or adrenaline to bring meaning, every bit left until the only thing remaining was his mate. Elle.

"You think this is the ghetto, too?" she asked, voice hard.

She didn't notice the intense rightness coursing between them. It was so obvious to him, the disconnect threw him off.

Her foot started tapping an angry rhythm. "Calling a perfectly good neighborhood the ghetto because the population isn't all white. Well?"

Well, what? Oh! "No, I don't think this is the ghetto. Great neighborhood." *Get your brain out of your pants. Listen and answer. Basic politeness like your mama taught you.*

She rolled her eyes. "Don't patronize me. It's not the ghetto but it's not great. It's not even average."

He looked around at the lush trees and view of the not-so-distant Rockies. "It's better than mine." He could smack himself. Again. *Good idea. Tell the woman you live in a shithole. That'll make her want to visit.*

Elle blinked at him, her shoulders relaxing as if the comment surprised her and not in a bad way. After a moment, she offered a tentative smile and sat down. Then stood up again. "Do you have work you need to do? You don't need to babysit me."

But even as she said it, her fearful eyes surveyed the crowd again, looking for someone.

He sat, and she sat beside him, closer than two strangers usually would. He still held her elbow. He was touching his mate, and he didn't want to let go. "What happened?" Who did he need to chase down and sink his claws into so she could quit searching in apprehension?

Inhaling a shaky breath, she looked at her lap, embarrassed. "I think my blowtorch did it. I was hammering copper. The safety was engaged. I'm not sure how it happened."

He let her go to pull off his jacket. It put too much bulk between them and made him damn hot to boot. The movement gave him an excuse to look away as he said, "You were handcuffed to a bed at the time...." He hoped she'd take the prompt and run with it, but only silence greeted his statement. After a moment, he looked back at her. More fear shone in her eyes as she struggled to answer. "Ms. Montgomery, why were you handcuffed to your bed?"

"Call me Elle." Her voice was quiet. Finally, her chin jutted up. "Why are most people handcuffed to a bed, Mr. Hunt? It's self-explanatory."

His wolf roared in jealousy, and he swallowed it back with great effort. He had no right to be jealous, and she was lying anyway. Why? "I've heard handcuffs and boots have a following, ma'am, but my understanding is those boots look a little different than the ones on your feet." Although she looked damn sexy in welding boots, with her long legs and rocking curves. Oh, yeah, handcuffs and those boots worked for him abso-fucking-lutely.

Focus, Hunt. The woman had nearly died and most of her apartment had burned. Drooling on her like a whelp wasn't going to help her feel better or help him figure out whom to protect her from.

She actually laughed. "Am I under investigation? Is this formal or informal questioning?"

Maybe if he was blunt this would work better. He sucked at dancing around issues anyway. "Somebody tried to kill you. Who?" He leaned in closer. "I'll take care of it." Too aggressive? He meant it. Somebody tried to kill his mate. They were puppy chow.

She patted his knee, like he wasn't serious. "You're sweet."

He snorted and leaned away. "I don't think anyone's ever accused me of sweetness before." Asshole was a more apt description. The things his packmates had called him—rightly so—when he'd left…. He shook his head, tossing off the memories like a wolf shook off water. A different life under an alpha who'd driven the Tao pack to Hell. As a member of Magnum's inner circle, he'd made choices he couldn't atone for. He'd left so he wouldn't be that man anymore. But if she needed violence, he knew how to commit high levels of it, and he'd do it again, for her.

Her eyes widened as she held his gaze, seeming to grasp how deadly serious he was. "I suppose it's because you just saved me from a fire, but I feel safe with you."

The mate bond. She didn't feel it like he did, not a settled piece of life's puzzle mystically snapped into place. But maybe she felt some trace of it. He could work with that. He took her fingers, those damn welding gloves of hers still separating them.

The cat hissed at him, and she took her hand back to rub the scruff of its neck. He narrowed his eyes at the cat, trying to convey in a glance that she couldn't win this fight.

Elle didn't notice. "Would you...." She laughed again, nervously. "This is the oddest question, but would you ever consider hiring out as a bodyguard? In a week or so I have a commission coming in. I'll be able to pay starting then."

Her bodyguard? Excitement coursed through him. *Hell yes.* That was possibly the best idea he'd ever heard. He nodded, but she wasn't looking at him and kept talking. "I need to find a safe space to work until then. I'll practically sleep there until this piece is done. In about a week, I'll get the money, and then I can pay you a good fee. Just for a few weeks until...." She trailed off, once again scanning the people around them. "Or for longer." She looked away again, her cheeks darkening further in what must be a blush. "It's a crazy question, I know."

Yeah, if crazy meant perfect. He would start today, not in a week. "Ms. Montgomery—"

"Elle." Her sweet eyes turned back to him, her curls bouncing around her face like a lion's mane, making her look playful and bold and so very desirable.

"Elle. Yes. You can hire me." *Or I'll do it for free because it's my job to protect you.* He didn't say it, too inappropriate. He looked up at the drifting smoke centered on her apartment. Most of the building would be all right. Not her part. "Do you need a place to stay tonight?"

She stilled and shrank back, her initial enthusiasm waning quickly at the offer.

Huh. "No, not like...I'll stay on the couch. Your apartment is not going to be livable. You say you need a bodyguard. If you need a place to stay, stay with me. You can have the bed. I'll take the couch. I could use the company. In the building. Not in the bed." He was rambling something terrible, but she didn't shrink away anymore. She listened, her expression opening up. He let the words keep coming out of his mouth, hoping to reel her back in. "All my friends here are drinking buddies. I need to stop drinking." *Because I found you.* "I don't have other people. I could use the...I already said that." He said it again anyway. "I could use the company. You're safe with me. Ask any of the firemen here."

She nodded slowly and looked from one man in yellow to another. She'd ask, which meant she was considering his offer. "You're going to be able to be a good bodyguard? Alcohol not going to be a problem?"

He shook his head. "No. It's not a—" That was a lie. He ducked his head. "It's a bit of a problem. I can beat it."

Her hand landed on his shoulder. She'd taken off the gloves, and her hand felt too cold. Shock still had her. He looked up. Her eyes didn't hold censure. She kept his gaze steadily, assessing him. The fear she'd carried still hung heavy on her. Trusting a stranger was risky, but whatever she feared must be worse. He needed to find out what had happened.

She shrank away. "Let's meet tomorrow. We can

talk about an arrangement. I don't have the money to hire you for another week anyway."

Unacceptable. Wait...he'd read about something in a book once. What was the phrase? "Be my sober friend. I'll work for free if you remind me to stay clean. Then we can talk about payment when your commission comes in."

She glanced around the yard again, still searching for the man Adam had vowed to bite in half. She didn't flinch. He wasn't here. Elle clung to her cat and stared down at her safe. To his shock, she said, "I'll take the couch. I am going to ask around before leaving with you, but provided I don't hear anything, you have a deal." Her hand came out.

He took it. "Deal. Except I'm taking the couch." Before she could protest, he shook.

Chapter Two

A year and a half later....

"It's your night off, Adam. Get out of here. Go do something fun." Elle bent over in a pair of jeans with an enticingly located hole in the thigh.

Adam tried not to stare at the swath of walnut skin between the light denim of her jeans and the hint of pink lace at the curve of her lovely ass, but he couldn't find the willpower to turn away. So he did the next best thing. He told her. "Woman, I'm trying not to stare at your butt, but have you noticed the giant rip in those jeans?" He'd seen almost every inch of her by this point. Almost. Never all at once. Never in a way that invited him to touch. Each time, it drove him a little more to distraction.

They'd been working together since the fire. In the interim, they'd moved from his apartment to a two bedroom down the hall until six months ago when they'd moved into her fancy digs halfway between Denver and Boulder. He'd quit his job with the fire department, sobered up, and they'd become not just boss and employee but friends. Best friends.

They were together and she was safe, but he needed to figure out a way to push the relationship further without blowing the good thing they had going.

She stood up and stuck her fingers into the hole, feeling for the edges. "Oh. That's bigger than I thought." She tossed him his keys and wallet, which he'd dropped by the couch before last night's episode of *The Flash*. Like they did every week, she'd sat on one side of the couch and he on the other with a good foot and a half between them as they ate bowls of pho and watched Barry Allen save the city again. "Think of me and my exposed ass fondly while you scoop up some lovely lady for the evening, 'kay?"

"I always think about your ass fondly, boss." Not just her ass, but every inch of her from her decorated toenails to her brilliant mind. The kind of mind with both the creative juice to craft works of art and the savvy business sense for her career to take off. And by "take off," he meant Lady Gaga wore her collection at the last Grammy's kind of success. It made him proud as hell to be part of her life.

Today, she stood in front of him in a tank top and those ratty, sexy-as-hell jeans, her curls pulled away from her face with a do-rag—a sure sign she planned to spend the evening working on her new jewelry collection for the spring line. She patted his cheek in the familiar way they'd developed, the kind where she touched him in friendly and impulsive ways and he kept his hands to himself so he didn't do something crazy like drop her onto the couch and lick a path from her jawline to the cleft between her breasts.

"Seriously. We people need time off. Take it."

Except he wasn't a person. Because she expected him to, he trudged to the closet and grabbed his favorite leather jacket, the one he always put on her when she rode on the back of his bike.

Oshun hissed at him as she stalked into the room, and he bared his teeth. She didn't swat at him, though, and he didn't growl. Apparently they were having a good day.

"Good man. I'm going to be locked up in my studio, and Billy's here. It'll be fine."

Adam shot a baleful look at the kitchen where Billy, the guard she'd hired for his nights off, made himself a sandwich. If anything dangerous enough to make his paycheck warranted had occurred in the past year and a half, Adam wouldn't let anyone else watch over Elle, no matter what she thought he needed. But the guy who'd handcuffed her to the bed hadn't made a move since the fire. Adam wasn't sure if the presence of a bodyguard kept the asshole away or if the asshole had given up. Regardless, about nine months into their arrangement, at her mulish insistence, he'd let her hire somebody else for one night every two weeks. It took him another three months to do more than walk around the block. Now he'd relaxed enough to drive the ten minutes it took to get to wildlands where he shifted and ran.

Getting back in touch with his wolf rejuvenated him. He'd never gone so long without shifting before he'd met her. "Call if you need anything." He kept the phone collared to his neck where he'd feel if it rang. So far she'd never called, but he'd never forgive himself if something happened to her while he chased rabbits or something equally animal.

His mate was beautiful and brilliant, and he was her guardian wolf, waiting patiently until the moment he could be something more.

It was ridiculous for Elle Williams, jewelry designer, to have a permanent bodyguard like a rock star or congressman. The thought of letting Adam go, though, physically hurt. Elle couldn't imagine life without his slow smile or deadpan sarcasm, and she didn't want to. So she paid him well enough that he stayed.

She slid her hand onto the small of Adam's back and escorted him to the door. His nights off were the worst. Billy came highly recommended from a well-regarded service, so she knew, logically, she was safe with him. Besides, Phillip hadn't contacted her in so long she thought maybe he'd given up.

Maybe.

The thought of his unnatural eyes still haunted her at night. Sometimes knowing Adam slept a few feet down the hall was the only thing keeping the nightmares away.

At the door, he lingered, messing with his pockets, and she lingered beside him, letting him pretend he wasn't wasting time. Why he wasn't anxious to get some freedom from the monopoly she had on his time mystified her. At first she'd thought he still worried about falling off the wagon, but he'd been clean for months. He deserved more out of life than to be shut up with her.

After he'd dug every imaginary piece of lint out of his pocket in a ridiculous attempt to look busy, she put her arms around him in a hug. If she didn't send him off, he'd never go. "Good-bye, Adam."

He enfolded her in his strength. His arms were amazing, so firm and beautifully sculpted. His face wasn't hard to look at, either, tan and broad with deep-set eyes and a jawline emphasized by soft stubble not quite long enough to be a beard but with more oomph than a five o'clock shadow. His honey-colored hair went from near brown in the winter to almost platinum by summer's end. Oh, and his eyes, the blue of noon skies, she found herself getting a little lost in them on occasion.

Sometimes she wished she'd met him in other circumstances, ones which might've included a date. Maybe more. But their friendship was better than the fickle dangers of a sexual relationship. If she'd learned anything from Phillip it was that trusting your libido over your good sense led to more danger than she'd ever imagined. People changed in a relationship. She couldn't stand the thought of Adam changing.

"You okay?" he asked, his voice rumbling through his broad chest.

She still had her arms wrapped around him. *Great.* She laughed and pulled back so she could see his eyes. "Just want you to remember who you're coming home to." *Because I'm too selfish to let you find a real girlfriend.*

A slow, lopsided grin made his handsome face devilish. "Like I could forget...." With one hand he tugged up on the waistband of her jeans. Before she could figure out why, his other hand smacked her on the ass—her bare ass. He'd repositioned the hole. "When I have this to come back to."

Her butt cheek smarted from the slap, and her

breath picked up. Suddenly, the firmness of his chest and heat from his body pressing against hers took on a whole new meaning. Cool air replaced his hand as the fabric dropped back into place, and the wildest desire took hold of her. She wanted him to put his hand right back and squeeze.

Employee. He was her employee. And they were friends. Doing something like this would fuck up the best relationship she'd ever had. She didn't even want sex, not after Phillip. It was too messy and complicated and beyond what she felt ready for. But maybe a kiss.

She squeezed her legs together, trying to stymie a need she hadn't felt outside her wicked imaginings since her whirlwind affair with Phillip. Oh God, was she biting her lip?

Adam's gaze darkened as his arms tightened around her. Dammit, she needed to quit giving him signals—to stop flirting, stop being confusing. She forced a laugh and pushed away, and he let her leave the warm circle of his arms. She took another step back, out of reach and at a distance far less friendly than their usual closeness. It made her sad. She needed to get them back on firm footing. Another laugh, like the tension amused her. "Somebody does need to get laid. Have a good night." Another step away. She couldn't look him in the eye, and that wasn't like her. She forced her gaze back up. His lips parted like he had something to say but it wouldn't come out.

He nodded and left without a good-bye.

Adam ran. His wolf threatened to blast through

his skin and turn him back around to his mate in a full-press charge. He couldn't let it; Elle hated aggression. He hopped onto his motorcycle and peeled out, throttling forward with an intensity he'd never felt before. He barely made it out of the urban sprawl, barely into the safety of the open plains when he let his bike turn to the side and skid into the brush. He launched off his seat, shucked his jacket and pants, and let the wolf out as he sprinted as fast as he could away from the woman he loved.

***

Despite the evening breeze, the heat of Elle's workshop stifled her. The air coming off the mountains did nothing to cool the sweat from her forehead—or tame the fire in her insides.

She'd spent ten minutes soldering a corner that should've taken two. With a disgruntled breath, she reached for her water bottle, but a scant few drops hit her tongue before it was empty.

"Fine...." she muttered and shut everything off. She'd never once left the room with something on, not since the apartment fire. Sometimes she still wondered if Phillip had set it or if it'd truly been an accident.

Not that she'd feel better about him either way.

She unscrewed her bottle cap and headed for the kitchen, the air conditioner, and maybe a scoop of the praline ice cream in the freezer. Adam had never tried her favorite flavor before meeting her, but upon consumption of one bite had insisted they always keep it on hand.

He was funny that way, quick to make decisions

but faithful to them anyway. She'd always been so cautious, Phillip being a notable exception—and look where that had gotten her.

So many times she'd wanted to tell Adam what had really happened, but how did she say, *I dated a werewolf,* without sounding like a lunatic?

Lunatic. Affected by lunar events. Like a lycanthrope. She shook her head. Sometimes she wondered if she'd imagined it herself, like a weird effect of smoke inhalation or something. Then she'd think about that cold look in his eyes. The prickly way his fur—his *fur*—had felt against her cheek. No. Werewolves were real. She shivered. She'd tried to find out more about them, but sorting fact from fiction on the Internet had proved impossible. She'd looked for cryptologists and other so-called experts in esoteric fields, but the few she'd found seemed more kooky than reliable. In the end she'd given up, discontent with her ignorance but not sure what else to do.

The cool air and lemony smell of the kitchen brightened her spirits. Water or ice cream? She stared at the refrigerator, debating whether to open the freezer or press her bottle against the dispenser. Maybe she'd stay up for Adam and eat ice cream with him. Hopefully whatever he did tonight would help ease the weird spike of tension between them.

The thought of him with another woman made her shoulders clench and her fingers tighten around the water bottle.

She stretched her neck to one side and then the other. She was his boss not his girlfriend. She had zero right to stop him from seeing dozens of women.

Water now. Ice cream later with Adam. She

didn't think she'd be going to sleep any time soon anyway, and if he came home smelling like perfume, she'd need the comfort of frozen calories.

Not that he'd ever come home smelling of another woman. Whatever he did without her, he managed to be discreet about it, and she appreciated that.

In the movie room, next to the kitchen, Billy watched TV or did something else not particularly bodyguard-like. Right after the fire, she'd wanted someone—okay, she'd wanted Adam—in her sights at all times. Now she'd gotten more lax. The fear had faded into something not quite so desperate, even if it never completely went away.

The voices in the other room weren't accompanied by a soundtrack, which was weird. She stopped her cup before tapping the water dispenser, her hyper-vigilant gut telling her to stay silent and listen. Just in case. As she focused on the sound it became clear that the TV wasn't on. Somebody else was in the room with Billy. Another man.

Cold slid up her back, tensing her muscles in the beginning of fight, flight, freeze. She couldn't hear the voices clearly enough to distinguish anything other than they were murmuring calmly. Billy wasn't ordering this guy to leave or panicking about a gun or anything. They were calm, so it must be a friend or relative—somebody he'd let in. He wasn't supposed to have anybody at her house, but it was human nature to break rules, and she made it easy to do by locking herself up in her shop for hours on end. She should go to the room and confront him about the breach of contract.

Except every instinct inside her said to escape.

Adam. She needed Adam. It wasn't rational and it wasn't fair, but it didn't matter. He kept her safe. Feeling like a total wuss, she texted him. She wanted to be a brave woman and check it out for herself, but she paid Adam to assess threats so she didn't have to. He took his job seriously, and he'd want her to contact him, even on his night off. No sense being that girl who went toward the noise when she should be heading out the door. She set her water bottle down as quietly as she could and ducked out the sliding glass door to the side yard.

Oshun shot out after her, fur bristling as she clambered up a tree. Normally Oshun spied on strangers from the highest perch she could find, staring down at them with wide and watchful kitty eyes until she decided they were safe. Not this time. If Oshun thought they should run from the man, Elle should heed the warning. She checked her phone. No response from Adam.

Okay. Get away on her own. She looked up into the tree where Oshun had scampered. *Stupid cat*. Elle couldn't leave her for werewolf meat.

Shit. She went to the opposite side of the tree where she wasn't visible from the house.

"Oshun! Come down here!" she whispered, motioning for the animal to come to her.

After a brief glance her way, Oshun continued to watch the house, claws latched into the bark of the tree.

Of course calling didn't work. Oshun was a cat. Ignoring the dictates of human guardians was the cat way. Elle swung up onto the lowest branch of the tree. "I am seriously replacing you with a dog."

Oshun turned a longer glance back, eyes dilated,

her over-sized ears swiveling independently like mini-radar, before she resumed watch on the house.

"Yeah, you're right," Elle admitted. "I love your stubborn, fuzzy ass too much."

She reached the crook in the tree where Oshun had set up sentry. Maybe she should stay up here, too. Most people didn't look up, right?

Shoulders tense, breath shaky, she talked herself out of the creeping panic. She was making a big deal out of nothing. Billy had a brother who'd stopped by to borrow money or a boyfriend who'd come over for a quick snog or something totally normal, and Adam would come home to find her hiding in a tree with a cat. They would spend the next year and a half laughing about this.

She stroked Oshun's tan fur, taking comfort in its softness. The cat didn't acknowledge her existence. "We should get out of the tree and go...somewhere." She checked her phone. Still no word from Adam. Where was he?

Hadn't she told him to go get laid? Dammit. He was fucking some other woman, and she was stuck in a tree with her cat. Anger replaced some of her fear, but she wasn't sure whom to direct it at—him for having normal human needs or herself for wanting to deny him those needs so she could keep him at her beck and call. Who cared if it made her a selfish bitch? Next time he said he didn't need a day off, she'd hold him to it. Her skin tingled as she thought about his hand smacking her ass and the strength of his chest as she'd leaned against him. If he had needs, she could fulfill them. It would be weird and possibly wonderful, and they'd find a way to stay friends afterward, right?

The fantasy of finally seeing Adam in all his naked glory, of touching him and not worrying about the consequences, heated and loosened her tense muscles and replaced her apprehension with a desire she couldn't slake. Grumbling, she pried Oshun off her perch. The cat fought her, clinging to the branch. "We're leaving, idiot cat." They would find Adam, return home so he could kick out Billy's friend, and then she'd fire Billy. Afterwards, she'd spend an itchy night imagining what it'd be like to drag Adam into her room to relieve this aching tension.

"Going where, mate?" Phillip's voice replaced the heat with ice, and she froze in place.

He walked across her yard from the kitchen. The house lights backlit him with a golden halo and left his face in shadow, but his eyes glowed with the same amber light that haunted her nightmares.

Her ex was back. In her house. Horror ripped a hole in her sweet imaginings. Her skin prickled and fingers dug into the tree like she had claws of her own. "Get off my property," Elle ordered, forcing her voice to stay steady. Oh yeah, she looked large and in charge, arguing with a treed cat. A steady voice would totally impress him.

Not.

He stalked forward with the sinewy grace of the wolf he hid inside.

"I told you to leave." If only her voice would stay strong, but panic rode her so hard she could barely keep her footing.

He leapt onto a low branch with inhuman dexterity, bringing his head level with her knees. "And I told you that we're forever, mate."

Oshun hissed and swatted. Claws left a trail of

blood across his pretty-boy face.

He growled, grabbed the cat by the scruff, and flung her off the tree.

"Oshun!" Rage exploded as she watched her cat land on the ground. If he hurt the cat, she'd kill him. "Mother fucker!" She balled her fist and jabbed Phillip in the nose, like Adam had taught her.

Phillip's expression blanked in surprise as his head snapped backward and he fell to the ground.

Elle hustled out of the tree and ran to Oshun.

The cat rotated and lurched to standing, took a few unsteady steps, but seemed okay. *Thank god.* "Run, girl!" She'd follow the cat. Oshun, good girl, dashed off toward the road, running in an almost-straight line. Elle followed. She'd gotten to CU Boulder from Los Angeles on a track scholarship and now plied every ounce of her willpower into the sprint.

A motorcycle roared in the distance. Adam? *Oh, please let it be Adam.*

What did she expect him to do against a werewolf? She'd grab the cat and get on the bike and they'd speed away. That's what they'd do.

Then she'd call the security company and get Billy fired. Or press charges. Her hired bodyguard had let Phillip inside to kidnap her. What the fuck?

Anger made her faster. She pointed toward the sound. Even if it wasn't Adam, she'd hitch a ride from whomever she found and call Adam from somewhere safe.

No noise alerted her to Phillip's presence, so the leap took her by surprise. He knocked her off her feet, and she landed face first in the dirt. Rocks jammed into her sternum, and her hands stung from impact.

Phillip's weight landed heavily on her back, forcing her to the ground. "I like it when you run, mate." His hot breath misted against her cheek. "I like to chase you."

"Get off me!" She struggled, pushing up with her back.

His grip closed painfully around her wrist, wrenching her hand behind her. "I tried to do this nicely. Tried to woo you like a human. But you didn't listen. So this time I'll take you like a wolf."

She bucked, flailing to get him off of her. But his relentless grip held on even as his voice stayed soothing, hushing her with whispered sounds that meant nothing. Phillip was a monstrous psychopath. And he'd found her.

Chapter Three

Adam sped down neighborhood streets at highway speed, praying to whatever gods may or may not exist that he'd be back in time. *Fucking service bodyguard.* He was never taking a night off again.

With his keener-than-human vision, he spied Oshun picking her way through rocks near the road. Elle would want the cat. He veered off course. The cat ran. He scooped it up, ignoring the claws and fangs digging into his forearm.

If Oshun was here, Elle would likely be outside, too. He stopped the bike to assess the surroundings and unceremoniously stashed the cat in a saddlebag. While moving, the sound and smell of the motorcycle overpowered everything else. Stopped, he got his ears and nose back.

Wolf. Another werewolf roamed nearby. A male. The hair on the back of Adam's neck stood on end as the instinct to protect his territory and challenge the interloper ground into him. He wanted to shift and charge after the invader.

Elle would freak out. He needed to stay human.

A scream fractured the night. Elle? *Fuck.* He hit the accelerator, taking his bike off the road and into the grasslands.

A quarter mile in, he found Elle on the ground, face in the dirt with a werewolf crouched on her back. Rage coursed through Adam, and it took every bit of will he possessed to stay human as he stopped the bike.

The werewolf glared at him, eyes full of menace and possessive lust. "Mine."

Oh hell no. Adam growled and jumped him. They rolled off of Elle and onto the dirt.

The man stank of silk, cologne, and hair gel. Rich wuss. Adam punched him in the stomach and pinned him with a knee against his chest. "Not yours. Not even close." *She's mine.*

Elle scrambled up and backed toward the bike. "Adam, he's not…. You have to be careful. Let's go."

Beneath his hands, the man started to shift. Adam saw two choices, shift and shred this asshole's furry carcass across the prairie—which would be great until Elle ran screaming into the night—or get her out of here.

He wanted to kill the guy for touching his mate—for touching any woman when she didn't want to be touched. The guy deserved it.

But Elle was panicking so hard he could smell her terror. *Take care of her first. Take care of the asshole later, when Elle doesn't have to watch.* "Get on the bike," he ordered. He sprang back as the man morphed into a silver wolf.

Faster than human, he straddled his motorcycle. Elle grabbed his waist, hugging him tightly in her fear, and they took off.

The wolf chased behind, jaws snapping at their heels, and Adam hit the accelerator. Wolves were fast, but not as fast as a tricked-out motorcycle. A few more seconds, and they'd left the wolf behind.

As Elle clung to him, her body shaking with emotion, he realized why she'd never told him from whom she was running. She didn't think he'd believe her if she said she'd dated a werewolf.

What was Adam thinking? Phillip had changed right in front of him. As the adrenaline wore off, Elle pressed her cheek against Adam's back and worried about what would happen next. Would he freak out and leave because she hadn't told him what he was up against? She'd put him in a lot of danger with ignorance.

On the other hand, who in their right mind would've believed her?

The motorcycle slowed. They'd only been going for ten minutes or so. As far as she was concerned, they could drive all night and it wouldn't be far enough. It soothed her to rest with her arms around Adam's thick chest and hang on.

But she owed him an explanation. They came to a stop at a gas station. He turned off the engine and put his feet down but otherwise didn't move.

"I can fill it up," she whispered, but she didn't move either. She swallowed the nervous lump in her throat and hung on, hoping it wouldn't be the last time she got to be close to Adam.

Finally he twisted to look at her, his expression serious but otherwise unreadable behind the motorcycle glasses. "We stick with cash. I'm going to get some at the ATM here, and that's the last plastic transaction until we have a better plan."

She slid her own ATM card out of her phone case. "Use mine." It wasn't his job to take care of her financially.

But he shook his head. "In case he's looking, mine's less likely to attract his attention." He cupped her jaw with his hand, the first sign he wasn't mad. She leaned into the touch, and he ran his finger along her jaw, carefully like she was delicate. "Have you eaten? My guess is no. You forget to eat when you're working."

Until he'd mentioned it, she hadn't been hungry. Suddenly, she was ravenous. She eyed the gas station speculatively and tried to make a joke. "Think they carry organic?"

He laughed. "No. Prepare for a hot dog." He smiled as he stowed his helmet and glasses, and she felt so much better. Life may be crashing around her, but they were okay, and nothing else mattered nearly so much. "Come on inside with me."

She swung her foot over the saddle and a new worry hit her. "Oshun!"

A pitiful meow sounded muffled, and Adam tapped a saddlebag. "One miserable cat, safe in the bag."

He'd saved Oshun. He hated that cat. She threw her arms around his neck and pulled him tightly to her. His arms came around her, comforting and strong, their ordeal erasing all of the weirdness of earlier. He smelled like leather and pine, the outdoorsy scent clean and clear. He never came home smelling like another woman. She didn't care about fairness; she liked to think of him as all hers. "Thank you. Thank you so much, Adam."

He stroked her back comfortingly. "It's my job. What next, boss?"

Get out of here. Find somewhere safe—if safe even exists. Pretend tonight didn't happen. "Drive. Just drive."

***

Elle is not going to like this place. Adam handed her a key to their cheap-ass motel room anyway, all he dared afford with cash on hand and no definitive plan for the future. Elle didn't want to go home tonight, and until he knew the whole story—and he figured out how to tell her the truth about himself— he was okay with that. When they traveled, though, she always booked rooms in bed-and-breakfasts or chichi little boutique places, the kind with character. Also the kind with a wall between their beds. This two-queen room promised to be as bland as every roadside chain motel in the country. He mostly hoped it was clean. He didn't want to think about the part where he'd spend the night a few uninterrupted feet away from her, trying not to stare at his mate as she slept.

She pushed the door open without a comment for the 1970s orange decor and dropped Oshun onto the first bed. The cat immediately ran under it.

The bed closest to the door was his; that way he'd encounter any incoming threats first. They'd work that out later. Now he needed answers.

"Did we pass Cheyenne?" she asked.

"About half an hour ago." He'd driven north toward the Black Hills, almost like his home called to him in times of stress. He wouldn't be welcome back.

Magnum Tao and his buddies weren't forgiving of those who left the fold. Sometimes he wondered if Drew Tao, Magnum's son, had ever come back to the town of Los Lobos to challenge his father. If Drew won, Adam might consider returning to see if he could earn his way back into the pack's good graces. He glanced at his mate. And to see if he could bring a human into Los Lobos. In the past, they'd been banned.

Sure, he could take on Elle's ex by himself, but the lack of desire to go back wasn't entirely about that asshole. The older he got, the more he missed his pack, and now that he had a mate, he wanted her to be a part of his family, to know him fully, wolf and all. That meant bringing her home to Los Lobos.

Elle sat on the bed facing away from him and pulled her knees to her chin. She looked so damn vulnerable, her strong arms wrapped around her shins, her hair wild as it rioted out from beneath her do-rag.

He sat next to her, and she leaned toward him as the bed shifted. He put a tentative arm around her shoulders. She leaned into it, and he curled her into his side. It felt natural to have her under his arm and tucked close. The last of the adrenaline from her ex's attack—from that asshole's claim on the woman Adam thought of as his own—faded into contentedness. He could sit like this for hours.

She snuggled her lithe body closer, wrapping him in her heady smell of fire and vanilla as she rubbed against him, and he realized sitting like this for hours would put him in a less contented and more needy frame of mind.

Hell, minutes would. He was getting hard, and

she hadn't done anything but touch him in friendly ways. He ignored the prickling desire coursing through him. Another aggressive male trying to paw her was the last thing Elle needed right now.

"I'm sorry for putting you in danger," she said.

"Facing danger is my job."

"Yeah, but I should've told you what you were really up against. I just didn't know how." She shivered and turned her face up to his. Her eyes filled with distress, and her expression turned disgusted. "He's a monster. He turns into an animal. He did it in front of me the night you and I met. It was horrible." Her words cut him, and he didn't know how to respond. Would she think the same thing of him if he told her about himself? She kept talking, each word another knife. "It's not like he actually loves me, either. Not really. He kept calling me his mate, making me the only one fate would let him have."

Adam's spine stiffened. *My mate. Not his.* "He called you his mate?" She couldn't be. Was it even possible some other wolf felt the same claim? "Did he use that exact word?"

"Yes! Isn't that nuts? I don't know if a mate is a-a werewolf thing,"—she spit out the word "werewolf" with the horror usually reserved for war and terminal disease—"or just part of his crazy. How awful to believe you're forced to be with somebody? Like you have no choice in the matter." She shook her head again and snuggled closer to another, in her estimation, horrible monster. "How fucked up is that for me or any other woman to have some monster obsessing over her? It's not even love; it's instinct."

Anger made his fists ball. The asshole had really done a number on her, making it impossible for her to see what a beautiful thing a mate bond could be. "You're not his mate."

"That's what I told him!"

"Mates aren't about control. Or they shouldn't be."

Her back shot straight as she stared at him like he'd lost his mind. "You're not defending his crazy, are you?"

"No! He's psychotic. I'm just saying...." What was he saying? Now wasn't a great time for a full confession. He pulled her into his lap, trying not to trap her with his arms, but he needed to be closer to her. Her weight felt good settled against him. Her closeness centered him. He put his temple next to hers and breathed her in, wishing he could communicate with touch instead of having to find the right words.

She didn't slide away. Instead, her tension eased as she released a small laugh. "You must be worried about me."

He blinked. "Huh?" Worry nearly consumed him.

"Last time you put me in your lap was the first day we met, after you pulled me out of the fire, remember?"

He hugged her tighter at the memory of how he'd almost lost her before he'd even met her. Because of another werewolf. "Yeah. I remember."

She stiffened. He needed to let her go. She wasn't his to touch. Not yet. Maybe not ever if he couldn't convince her most werewolves were decent folk.

Before he released his embrace, she relaxed and put an arm casually around his shoulders. A light pressure against his grip asked for space, but her arm around him assured him she wasn't going far. He eased up, and she patted his chest. Her touch stuck with her usual friendly way, and he loved it as much as it ramped up his desire for more, confusing him. God, he wanted her.

"What were you trying to say?" she asked.

Her palm flattened against his right pec, and he had no idea what she was talking about. He only wanted her to keep touching him. "What?"

Her fingers tapped against him as her voice stayed calm, helping him think. "You said Phillip's psychotic. I agree." His enemy's name. Good to know. If he got the last name from her, he could track that motherfucker down. "You said something, and it sounded like you were defending werewolf mates. Is this your imagination, or do you have some relevant experience?"

Okay, so now may not be the time to bring up his own species classification, but maybe he could ease her into the idea. "I used to live near werewolves." That was absolutely true. "They weren't like him."

Her mouth opened in surprise. "This whole time you knew they were real? Damn. I would've told you a long time ago." She sagged. "How do you know your werewolves aren't the odd ones? Vegetarian werewolves or whatever, while Phillip is normal?"

He laughed. "There aren't vegetarian werewolves. W-*They* eat meat. But they don't eat humans," he added quickly. He stroked her back, soothing himself as much as he soothed her with the contact. "Werewolves are like people. Some are good and some aren't. You can't paint every wolf with the same brush."

Both palms went to his chest, and she studied

him intensely. "They're still monsters, too strong and too fast for a human to keep up with. And the way they change has to be magic. Now that Phillip's back, you're in danger. More danger than I ever told you. And I should have." She swallowed heavily. "If you want out of your contract, I understand."

"No. No, *hell no*." And leave her to Phillip's psychosis? Like he'd ever let that happen. But he needed to convince her werewolves weren't all monsters.

She closed her eyes, face relaxing in relief. "Thank you." She snuggled up against him again, pressing her body into his, and his body stiffened in response, the wolf raging at him to soothe her with his touch. Naked touch. If he claimed her right, she wouldn't have to be afraid because Phillip would know she was off-limits.

Wolf logic. Not human. Elle didn't think that way. He shifted, trying to find a more comfortable position that wouldn't alert her to his growing problem. "You're welcome."

Her voice turned shaky. "Phillip said since he couldn't woo me like a human, he'd take me like a wolf. I told you, this mate thing is crazy."

"Take you like a...." Anger simmered through him again. "He got it wrong. When it comes to mating, females are in charge. It's the same for wolves and werewolves."

She didn't say anything, and he couldn't tell if she believed him or not.

He scooted back against the wall, hauling her with him until they leaned together against the wooden headboard. After a year and a half, he finally knew her big secret. Now, maybe, he could get the whole story. "Tell me what happened."

Her dark eyes searched his for a moment, as if she still feared his response. Instead of brushing him off, though, she took a deep breath and finally started talking.

Chapter Four

E lle had *that dream* again. Not the terrifying one where she woke up screaming as Phillip shifted on top of her, smothering her in stiff, choking fur. Considering the day she'd had, that nightmare should've filled her night. But no, she dreamed the other one, the one where the fire raged and she was handcuffed to her apartment bed. Adam burst into the room, alone this time, wearing his fireman's pants and suspenders and nothing else. In three strides, he made it across the room and kissed her tears away. She snapped a suspender against his firm chest, and he tossed her on the bed—because in dreams handcuffs conveniently disappeared and reappeared as needed. She reached into his fireman's trunks to wrap her fingers around his thick shaft. His mouth sucked her breast, sending hot desire aching through her body. The fire raged around her and inside her, totally out of control.

She woke up, eyes snapping open on a gasp, her body hot and wet and wanting him. Unlike every other time she'd woken from *that dream*, though,

Adam lay behind her, his arm wrapped protectively around her midsection. With his body keeping her warm, the dream wouldn't let go, and she wanted to touch herself, to ease the ache in the way she usually did.

Hell, she wanted Adam to ease the ache for her. He was *right there.*

They must've fallen asleep last night as they discussed ex-boyfriends and girlfriends, laughing at old stories until the horror of the evening faded into comfortable friendship in a cheap motel room. The accommodation was small and grimy, like the old days before she'd made it. Unlike the old days, they'd shared a bed. Adam's body pressed against her back, from his leg wrapped over hers to his face nuzzled against her neck. The lingering kisses of her dream made her skin too sensitive, experiencing every sleep-addled touch like a heated caress.

Yes. She wanted him. If she was honest, she had for a while. But he was her rock. The risk of moving their relationship into a new realm still felt too dangerous. She couldn't lose him merely to live out sex fantasies with a hot fireman.

He sighed, his breath gentle against her neck.

She squeezed his hand. She needed to get up and slip out of bed before he awoke, but it would be so easy to turn around and wake him up with a kiss. Where had he gone for his night off? She hadn't asked why he'd come back with one less shirt than he'd left in, a fact she hadn't noticed until late into last night's confessions. The answer was obvious, even if he didn't smell like someone else. How else did you lose a shirt? She wondered if he saw the same woman every time or if he picked up a new stranger.

Not her business. The idea of another woman made her jealous enough to slide from the comfort of his arms and stumble to the coffeemaker, an old-fashioned drip style with a carafe big enough to caffeinate a party's worth of hangovers.

Adam is not mine, not mine. She plugged the thing in, scooped grounds into the filter, and puttered to the bathroom for water, contemplating jealousy. Adam was a man. He had needs. If she wasn't willing to satisfy them—or he wasn't interested in her satisfying them which, up until last night she'd believed to be true—then she couldn't be jealous when he went somewhere else.

The shower looked like heaven—a tiny, cracked, baked-in-dirty heaven. While the coffee percolated, she constructed a makeshift shower cap out of towels and stepped under a tepid stream. At least the motel provided a sliver of free soap. Free soap and free coffee were necessities. Everything else was foregoable luxury.

She rinsed her panties and bra out and hung them over the curtain rod. The jeans and tank top she'd have to live with, but work-worn underwear was simply not doable. At least the lace would dry quickly. She needed new clothes but had no money. How much did Adam have? What were they going to do next? Should she call the police? Did an entity exist for policing werewolves?

Adam already knew about werewolves. Maybe he knew about a supernatural police team—slayers or hunters or whatever, who took care of paranormal problems. With a big sigh she turned off the water. If she'd known he knew about wolves, she'd have told him the whole story a long time ago.

Wrapped in a thin towel, she headed for the coffee. Adam now slept with a pillow against his chest, right where she'd been, and the sight made her smile. Maybe last night they should've made a plan instead of gossiped about their love lives, but the laughter and camaraderie had been exactly what she'd needed.

She poured two cups, added dashes of sugar from an ancient canister, and took her first calming sip. Maybe she could find a hairdryer for her underwear. The closet?

Adam's coffee she put onto the nightstand next to him. It was eight in the morning, usually far past when he woke up for his morning workout. He'd want the caffeine first thing.

God, he was handsome as he slept. She needed to look for the hairdryer and get her clothes back on, but she couldn't resist watching him—just for a moment. Was it rational to be jealous of the pillow pressed up against him? Maybe not, but he stood up to monsters for her. He always had without knowing it. Now that he knew, he still stayed.

She pushed a lock of hair out of his eye, unable to resist touching him. His skin felt hot, even in the cold room, and it made her shiver. Her towel wasn't much protection against the elements in a motel where the heater sputtered and grunted and barely pushed air. She needed to go find that hair dryer. She wanted to crawl in bed next to him and wake him up with her mouth. Until yesterday, when he smacked her on the ass and sent her blood racing, it'd been easy to resist. She could tell herself he wouldn't want her to. But that one move told her he'd welcome any advances with open arms and eager lips.

The internal debate raged, her hand poised to touch his cheek.

His sleepy voice rumbled. "Gotta admit, you wearing a towel and serving me coffee in bed had never been a fantasy of mine." One eye opened, and he shot her a playful grin. "But I'll add it to the list."

He had fantasies about her? She dropped her hand to his shoulder. His skin burned through the sheet and T-shirt. How did he stay so hot in the frigid air? "Your fantasies are awfully tame."

He narrowed his eyes as the corner of his mouth rose dangerously. "Oh, that's just the beginning." He pushed up until he leaned against the headboard, sleepy eyes open and hair mussed like he'd been in a photo shoot. "It gets more interesting from there. You'd be thoroughly impressed."

His movement put her hand in his, a sweet touch for the devious light in his eyes. She couldn't believe she was about to say this, but the need for connection overwhelmed her. She trusted Adam. They'd figure it out. "Do you need a written invitation to show me? Or what are you waiting for?"

The shock on his face would make her laugh if she wasn't so keyed up. He looked her up and down slowly, his eyes narrowing and gaze growing more heated as he took her in.

She shrugged, teasing him. "I suppose I'll get a piece of paper, then."

"Don't you go anywhere," he practically growled. His big hands seized her, making her squeal as he tossed her onto the bed.

Her insides sizzled with nervous excitement as he rolled on top of her. She'd been avoiding this, not just with Adam but with anyone. Phillip had always been a little rough. Not badly so. Not until the end at least. But he was so strong. Giving over control had frightened her more and more as he'd grown more possessive and less stable.

No one should be afraid in a relationship. She'd known that. Finally, she'd gotten brave enough to leave.

As if Adam sensed her shifting mood, he paused and wound his fingers into her hair. Instead of going straight for a sexual touch, he stroked her cheek with his thumb. "I'm strong," he rumbled, his words somehow echoing her fears. His eyes held so much emotion when his gaze captured hers, as if it wasn't the first time he'd thought about them together like this. As if he'd held back for a long time, waiting for her. "But my strength is yours to command. Entirely yours. You tell me what to do, and I'll do it. You tell me to stop, and I'll stop."

The words were nice, but they were only words until he backed them up. She leaned up on one elbow, brow furrowed. "Then back off." It was a simple test and completely unfair given that she'd just told him to show her his fantasy. Phillip would've failed.

She barely registered his nod before his arms unwound from her and he retreated to lie beside her, one fist clenched and expression unreadable as he stared at the ceiling.

Gratitude swelled inside as she realized he'd meant what he said. She was safe. Adam had always been trustworthy in every way. He would be in this way, too. She leaned over him and cupped his jaw with her hand. His gaze found hers again, confused and hopeful. "Thank you. I just needed to see that."

She rubbed noses with him. "You might've noticed I carry a little baggage."

His arm came around her, and the other hand went back to her hair. "Anything you need." The raw intensity in his voice sent a thrill from her heart to her groin.

"I need a kiss."

He groaned, and she didn't wait for him to oblige her. She pressed her body against his hardness and took his mouth with hers. He answered her kiss with fevered ardor, matching her need with his own. His tongue traced the split of her lips, and she let him in. The desire flowing through her burned hotter than she'd realized, intense and immediate like it had been when boys were new and sex a mystery she needed to solve. She twined her fingers into his shirt, wishing it would vanish so she could touch him. His hands stroked her back and squeezed her ass, bringing her closer to him and stoking the fire between them.

Adam's touch was exactly what she needed, what she'd craved for so long. It almost scared her how badly. She broke the kiss, but her touch still roamed his body, exploring every rounded muscle and hard cut plane. "Don't leave after this. I still need you." She cringed as the last part came out. To *need* him sounded weak.

But he shook his head, relief in his eyes. "No. No, baby, I'm not leaving. We're a team."

She grinned, her own relief giving her peace. "I'm still your boss," she teased.

He smiled back, his face full of wicked goodness. "Then let me take care of you."

Adam held the most precious piece of his life, and his wolf wanted to howl for joy. So she hated werewolves and didn't know he was one. And yeah, they were on the run from her crazed ex-boyfriend. There was some shit to deal with. But Elle lay on top of him wearing nothing but a towel. Armageddon couldn't distract him from this moment. He kissed her again, toppling her to the side. She squealed and he pulled back to make sure she still felt safe and happy. Her devious smile shone up at him. Her fingers twined back into his hair.

Oh yeah, things were good. Better than good. Amazing. She wanted him. Life was perfect.

"Get this off," she growled, shoving at his T-shirt.

"Happy to." He let her yank the shirt up, and he pulled it over his head.

She scratched her short nails down his chest and tugged at the curls of hair. "I love this."

Good, because my body is yours. He couldn't tell her yet. He gripped her thigh and slid his hand up until he cupped her bare ass. "I love all of you." The confession was dangerously close to *I love you*, but, dammit, it was true. Fate may have decreed them to be mates, but they became best friends on their own. He'd grown to love her during their time together.

She clucked her tongue. "So serious. You look so"—she kissed his forehead then his chin—"very"—her lips touched his chest, once, twice, thrice, sending chills through him. He threw back his head, giving her better access—"serious." She pulled away, and it was all he could do not to grab her and pull her back against him. But her hands went to the knot of her towel, and he stopped, gaze glued to the too-slow motion of her hands.

"I think I can fix that," she whispered. The towel crept across her skin, revealing one dark inch at a time. His claws wanted to spring out and rip the fabric to shreds. She smiled, knowing exactly how crazy she made him, and he loved it.

"Woman," he warned.

She laughed and dragged the fabric across one nipple, baring it erect and gorgeous. He managed to pull his gaze up to hers and give her a dangerous smile. She grinned back.

He reached forward and slid his knuckles across her breast. She sighed and leaned in to his touch. He cupped the firm roundness, feeling the press of her hard nipple against his palm. She dropped the rest of the towel, her chin raised and eyes closed as she experienced his touch. He kissed her chin, down her neck to her sternum then gently lowered her to the bed.

Her hand ran down his side as he explored her with his mouth. The orange of the motel soap clung to her skin, but underneath she tasted of vanilla and spice. His Elle.

He wanted to howl in triumph. To nip her and run his face across her skin. His wolf wanted to claim her with a bite, to make sure any wolf out there knew she belonged to him. But he couldn't. She hated wolves. Would she—*could* she hate him? He should tell her before they did this.

And then she'd run away.

No. He found her nipple with his mouth, drawing her in and making her gasp. He didn't want to let her go. He needed her.

Her hands clutched his back, and she moaned his name. Would she still do that if she knew what he was?

Probably not. But if she found out later, after they'd made love? It would be worse.

"God, please, Adam. Don't stop." Her hand shot down his pants, grabbing his ass and squeezing.

He leaned up and took her mouth in a deep kiss. Her hands went wild, caressing him like she couldn't get enough as her tongue circled his, plunging and taking.

He broke away enough to whisper, "I need to tell you something."

"No condom? I didn't think about that." Her voice turned breathy as she kissed him again and again, her lips lingering on his chin as her tongue traced his jawline.

His libido skipped a step. Wolves didn't have to worry about unwanted pregnancy. Humans did. He could get her pregnant.

A staggering thought. Not that he minded the idea of a family. On the contrary, kids were part of his perfect future vision. *Future* kids.

She pulled back farther. "You have herpes? Something else I should know about?"

He blinked at her, the question taking him by surprise. "No." Wolves didn't have to worry about human diseases, either.

She tapped his nose. "Good. Then you should use that mouth for something other than talking. If we're not having sex, we're going to have to get creative."

That sounded like the best thing ever. "I like creativity."

Her hips shifted suggestively under his, rubbing her body against his erection in mind-bending circles. "Then shut up and show me something new."

Maybe if he gave her a fucking fantastic orgasm, she'd forgive him for being a wolf. She'd told him to quit talking, and she was his boss, so it was the only legit plan. Or so his addled brain insisted. He kissed a trail down her torso, stopping to give her breasts ample attention. She writhed under him, her body appreciative of his every touch. His mate was gorgeous and glorious and he had her underneath him.

"Don't stop, Adam, oh, God, don't stop."

Never stopping. Her thighs quivered as he pressed them apart, giving him access to her sex. Her hand wound into his hair as her hips thrust upward toward his mouth. With that encouragement, he dove in, taking her firmly with his lips. She screamed in pleasure as her sweet wetness coated his tongue. Heaven. Elle was heaven, and—at least for the moment—she was his.

Mind-blowing. Elle thrashed in pleasure as Adam took her with his mouth. His tongue drove her higher as his hands held her firmly in place, keeping her pinned for his ministrations. Every inch of her skin throbbed for his touch, her breath spun out of control, and she didn't think she'd ever get enough.

Why had they waited this long? Next she'd get her mouth on his cock and see how he liked the turnabout. She'd make him scream.

His tongue teased her, flicking across her clit in exactly the right way, and she clenched her fingers in his hair, urging him on. "Please, baby, just like that."

His thumb pressed into her core, filling her emptiness as his mouth continued its torture. She didn't want his thumb, dammit, she wanted him, his thick shaft filling her like he did in her dreams.

She'd missed sex; she recognized that now. But Adam was worth the wait.

His hand shifted, sending fingers inside her as his tongue continued its sweet rhythm. Her thoughts blurred as pleasure took over, sending her into that place where nothing mattered but sharing bliss with someone else. Maybe she screamed, maybe she cried his name, all she knew was her body was electrified, sending currents of energy through her emptiness, filling long-cold spaces with Adam's warmth.

This could be love, choosing and sharing and being together in trust and mutual desire. She tugged Adam's shoulder and he followed her demand, holding her against him in a full-body embrace as she shuddered down from the high.

"Elle," he murmured against her hair, his lips gentling her shoulder. "Elle, Elle, oh, my darling Elle."

She loved him.

The thought echoed in her mind, scaring her and yet filling her with light. What now? Did she tell him? Did she show him? She kissed him, and he kissed her back, tasting of what he'd done. His hands roamed her body, both lazy and desperate. She'd talk of love later. For now…. "Take your pants off."

He chuckled. "Yes ma'am."

She needed to feel him, taste him, give him the same release he'd given her. Then, equally satisfied, they could talk.

Anxious, she smoothed her hands down his rigid abdominals and sent her fingers into his jeans. He released the button, giving her better access. She caressed beneath the waistband of his boxers, feeling the soft skin between his hips. His erection bobbed against her knuckles, and he sucked in a breath.

"Shit." His hands pressed against hers, stopping her eager progress as his body stiffened in something other than lust. "Oh, shit."

"What?" She tried to shake off the haze, to respond to his alertness, but she'd nearly reached her prize.

Wait, was that the sound of motorcycles slowing?

His hands pressed harder, holding her in place. Yes. Those were motorcycles. Stopping outside their door.

Adam leaped up, moving so fast she could barely follow in her lusty haze. Jeans and her tank top landed in her lap. "Get your clothes on."

Her wet underwear still hung on the shower rod. She shoved on what he'd given her as he spied out the front window then motioned her forward. "Aren't we safer inside?"

"No. A single werewolf could break this door down easy, and there are five of them." His voice was still gruff from their activities, and she'd bet he sported a painful erection.

Damn Phillip and his terrible timing.

"We need to get out of here. As soon as the door opens, run for the bike. Start it and drive away." He crawled under the bed to a chorus of insane hissing.

"What about you? I'll get the cat." She knelt down, but he popped back up, an irate Oshun already gathered in his meaty arms. She took her cat. He'd need his hands to protect them.

"Hopefully, I'll be on it. If not, drive the fuck away. Bodyguard's orders." He glanced back at her, eyes bright in the dawn light shining in patches through the bedraggled blinds. "I'll catch up down the road."

Like hell he would. It wasn't just Phillip anymore. Shit, they were in trouble. She licked her lips and took his hand. "I'm not leaving you."

His hand cupped her cheek. "Elle, this is what you hired me for. Let me do my job." Before she could answer, he kissed her, his mouth firm and caring. She put her arms around his neck and pulled him closer, needing another moment. They were not going to end like this, not right when she'd finally figured out what she really needed from him.

He pulled away. "We have to surprise them if this is going to work."

She nodded. They were going to get out and back on the road together until they could figure out a real plan. And they would succeed, as long as they were together.

Adam opened the door.

Chapter Five

Five wolves in human form waited for them outside the door. Adam cursed under his breath. He'd been so distracted, he hadn't counted the sounds, just let them get jumped. Now Elle wasn't safe.

He would chastise himself later. Now he had to get them out of here. He spread his hands in a gesture of mock warmth. "Anything I can help you guys with?" Other than handing over his mate. He took a better look at each wolf in turn but stopped at the two who were obviously there for the muscle. "Craig? Jim? The fuck are you doing here?" They were from Magnum's circle, two lower-level flunkies who kissed ass and wreaked havoc on command. He couldn't picture them leaving Magnum's entourage to strike out on their own; neither one possessed the brainpower for it.

Jim laughed, his gelled hair flopping in time with the cackle. He still sounded more like a hyena than a wolf. "Adam Hunt. Fancy seeing your chicken-shit ass here."

Craig joined in the giggling. "Thought I smelled yellow."

Elle touched his back, her fingers light on his shoulder and waist. "You know these guys?"

"Yeah." And he could kick either one of their asses. Together, he could probably still take them. With three more wolves to help? That started to get problematic. "What're you doing so far from Magnum's leash? Last time I saw you, you were both well under his paw."

They both looked confused for a moment then Craig spit on the ground, disgusted. "You don't know."

"Don't know what?" He'd assumed they'd finally done something idiotic enough even the Tao pack leader couldn't stomach it, but the sour look on both their faces carried no shame or regret, only anger. Had something happened to Magnum? Despite the situation, a bud of hope formed in his chest. If Magnum was gone, maybe he could go home.

But they wouldn't let a human into Los Lobos. The hope died as soon as it formed. He wasn't going where Elle couldn't.

Phillip, now in a full Italian leather bike outfit, stepped forward. His sleek racing helmet rested in the crook of his arm. and his gaze took in Elle with a predatory look Adam wanted to rip off his smug face. "As fascinating as this reunion is, we've got business to attend. Adam Hunt, I've done a little research on you. Magnum's dead. You can go back and beg forgiveness of your enforcer. Hand over the woman, and we'll let you return to the Black Hills in one piece."

"What's he talking about, Adam?" Elle sounded

so afraid, like he'd actually consider their offer.

He grinned at her. "Long story. I'll tell you about it later, after we ditch these assholes. Get to the bike." And because it would piss Phillip off, he gave Elle a kiss. Her arm slid around him as she softened against him, the way he'd longed for since the day they'd met.

Phillip howled in rage and charged.

"To the bike," Adam ordered as he turned to catch the raging man. As soon as she rode out of sight, he could let his wolf out and have a shot at taking these assholes.

Phillip barreled into him. Adam sidestepped and tossed the man to the ground. If he could keep them coming one at a time—

Craig and Jim slammed into him at once. He sensed the changes more than saw them as the remaining men turned to wolves and leapt.

Elle screamed. The damn woman wouldn't get the hell out of here.

Adam struck with precision, trying to keep too many men at bay. Someone got in a punch to the back of his leg, sending him to one knee. He grabbed two heads and knocked them together. Another kick to his gut sent him doubled over. The wolves were in now, mouths open, claws stretched.

Human skin tore easily beneath wolf teeth. Without his wolf, this would go badly.

One wolf whined and spun, snapping behind him.

Elle swung a tree branch like a bat.

"Get to the bike!" he yelled, as proud of her as he was pissed at her.

The wolf jumped for her. He grabbed its tail and pulled with every bit of his strength. The animal launched backward, bringing Adam onto the macadam beneath him.

"I'm not leaving you," Elle screamed back.

Another thump as she hit someone else.

He shoved the wolf off him and kicked at Jim, sending the man to the ground. Someone grabbed his feet, dragging him back over the broken pavement. He kicked out, but another man grabbed him, pinning him down.

Elle's bravery was admirable, but he needed her to leave. He couldn't win as a human. He wasn't sure he could win against this many even as a wolf, but he had a shot. If she stayed, he would die and Phillip would take her.

Which meant she needed to get the hell out of here, no matter the cost.

A painful realization hit him. She wouldn't stay if she knew what he was.

One of the wolves bared its teeth, wet jaws open to attack. Elle caught his gaze, her eyes widening. She raised that damn tree branch to attack as the other wolf prowled toward her.

She could still get to the bike. Despite how well she'd held her own, everyone seemed convinced she wasn't capable of taking care of herself. Their mistake.

The wolf swiped at his leg, drawing blood. He ignored it.

Heart in his throat, he shook his head at her. "I'm sorry," he mouthed as he shrugged off his jacket.

Her eyebrows slid together in confusion, the last look she'd ever give him before she found out she'd been living with a monster.

He started to shift. Her eyes widened in horror

as understanding dawned. She backpedaled, dropped the branch, and finally dashed for the bike.

She was leaving him. Good, right? He could focus on not dying. Watching her go, watching his heart run away, felt like drowning.

His attackers lost their grip as he shifted; he'd always been fast at it. His skin toughened. His jaws elongated into teeth. The transition always felt like a homecoming, but this time the pain of knowing he'd lost Elle made the feeling bittersweet.

The motorcycle started up. Phillip yelled for someone to stop her. A wolf leaped for her side.

Adam moved faster. He slammed the wolf to the ground, his muzzle catching it by the nape. A sharp shake and its neck broke. One thug down, three and a prissy-boy to go.

Jim and Craig let their wolves out, Jim with an agonizing slowness, Craig with a more efficient morph.

The third wolf slammed into him, and they rolled. He shoved the wolf off, circling for another attack.

To his left, Craig zeroed in, ready to join the fray.

Craig leaped. The motorcycle slammed into him, sending the wolf flying. Elle reached down and picked up his favorite jacket. "Get your ass up here." She circled him once, keeping the wolves at bay with his bike as Phillip screamed uselessly.

Adam launched himself up, transitioning as he went. Elle was already zipping forward by the time he landed behind her, naked and half-human.

She hadn't left.

"You should've told me," she yelled back as they sped down the empty highway.

"It's been a weird twenty-four hours," he yelled back as soon as his human vocal chords were working again. He tightened his arms around her and buried his face in her shoulders. She stiffened, afraid of him, but she hadn't left him to die.

He could work with that.

***

Nearly an hour and a hundred miles northeast, they stopped at the first copse of trees they'd seen in the vast plains of eastern Wyoming. A herd of honest-to-God buffalo meandered through grass tall enough to reach his hip. Somewhere on the road, he'd gotten his coat on, but it covered the least important half of him.

The damn cat, which Elle had stuffed back into a saddlebag before picking up the tree branch, had given up howling a good half hour ago, enduring in silent and somber dignity for once. Elle must be miserably cold without a bra and in those tattered jeans and a tank top. His wallet was back in the parking lot tucked into his pants. They were half-naked with no funds and no phones in the middle of nowhere.

With the motorcycle off, the only sounds were the chill wind in the grass, the low munching of the herd, and Elle's erratic breathing. He had no idea what to say to her. "I have to pee," he finally admitted in a grunt as he shoved off the bike. Elle pulled off the helmet, and her hair exploded into a riotous mane—he thought it looked fierce, but she'd hate it. She leaned over the handlebars, looking half-dead.

He turned back and dropped his jacket over her

shoulders. It wasn't doing him much good anyway with his dick swinging in the wind. She didn't move.

"Shit," he muttered. "Thanks for saving my ass." He stumbled off to relieve himself, unsure where to go or what to do next.

When he came back, she looked him up and down, and he was pleasantly surprised to see a hint of desire still sparked in her eyes. He leaned against the bike. "Not exactly the way I pictured you first seeing me naked." He sucked in a breath between his teeth and blew it out slowly. "But, hey, you're not ditching my wolfy ass here and leaving with my bike and jacket, so that's something."

"So you really are a...a...." The fear in her eyes cut him.

"You can say the word." It came out harsher than he wanted. He was furious at Phillip for what he'd done, not Elle for believing werewolves were bad after the only one she'd met turned out to be a fucking dickweed.

She looked away. "You're a werewolf. Like him."

"It's still me, Elle." He reached out slowly and touched her chin, trying to coax her back to face him. "We're not all—"

She kicked her leg over the bike and leaned into him. Her expression filled with a frustrated need he felt every time he looked at her, like he didn't know what to do with so much emotion. He pulled on the sides of his jacket, tugging her closer, and kissed her. Her arms came around him and her body sank against his, her worn-out tank top barely a whisper between her skin and his. The wind cut through the plains at ferocious speeds, but he didn't feel the cold. Elle held him, warming him up inside and out.

She pulled away, but her hands stayed locked around his neck.

"I wasn't expecting that," he managed to say.

She stood still, stiff as hell, not the same warm, friendly Elle she'd been before all this went down, but she wasn't running away either. He'd find a way to make it right between them. Her lips turned down in the overdone pout she used when harassing him. "I find your dick obnoxiously distracting."

He laughed. "*You* find it distracting? Try being me anywhere in your vicinity."

She puffed a breath of protest and pushed away. He didn't want to let her go, but he did. Making this right meant letting her dictate their physical relationship while she got adjusted to what he was. She started to take off his jacket.

"It's cold. Keep it."

Huffing pale breaths into the air, she slapped his jacket against his chest. "I wasn't kidding. I need you at least somewhat covered up if we're going to have a conversation."

He caught the jacket and couldn't help smiling. "Do we have to converse?"

She flipped him off, and he smiled harder, relieved. They were going to be okay. "So," she said carefully. "You come from a, uh, wolf pack in the Black Hills?"

"Yeah," he said, pulling the jacket on and tucking himself into it as best he could. "The Tao pack. Packs are usually named after their alpha. Pack leader."

She shrank back. "Alpha. That's...." She sucked in a breath. "I'm going to let that go for now. You were forced to leave because of some guy named Magnum who's dead now?"

He leaned against the bike, uncomfortable and not just because of the cold. "Sort of. Magnum was our alpha. He went a little crazy—no, a lot crazy—after his wife died. The things he made us do." He shook his head at memories he didn't want to recall. "They made me sick. He had all of us in his circle bullying the pack into submission, no matter the consequences. My big brother, Cam, was...he was awful, and I followed in his footsteps, tearing the pack apart with violence and fear. After Magnum's son left—was kicked out, actually. I wasn't supposed to know this, but Magnum had him blackmailed. But after Drew left, it got even worse. I did terrible things trying to impress Cam, and I can't take them back. Finally, I left, but leaving meant I couldn't return." He scratched his chin, his two-day stubble going on three days and getting long even for him. "If Magnum's gone, I wonder if Drew's back. He'd be a good leader, I think."

"So it's safe for you to go home?"

Where was she going with this? "Possibly. I did some things the others are unlikely to forget. I may not be welcome even with Magnum gone."

She frowned, thinking. "At this point, we're closer to South Dakota than to Denver. I didn't realize Phillip would bring a pack of wolves to find me. We need more of your kind to stop them." She put her hand on his shoulder, touch tentative but still comforting. "You were amazing back there, but five on one—two if you include me and a tree branch—isn't fair odds."

"They don't allow humans into Los Lobos. Nobody's supposed to know about us."

She snorted. "I already know about you. Taking

me there won't change anything. Besides, it's your...species that's attacking me. Where in the human world would I go? I have a werewolf problem. I need werewolves."

Her logic was sound, and, hell, he wanted to go home. He wanted to take her there and hopefully show her all werewolves weren't insane. If Drew was in charge, Los Lobos had a real chance at being some place good again, a place that would be safe to raise a family, maybe kids with Elle's curly hair and brown skin.

Okay, he might be getting a little ahead of himself, but now the thought had entered his head, he couldn't get it out. Elle could work from anywhere in the world; why not Los Lobos? She appreciated the country, adored animals—mostly her stupid cat, but Oshun would love the countryside—and everyone there would fall in love with her, just like he had.

No, not quite like he had. He took Elle's hand. She didn't stop him, but her expression turned so sad as she watched his fingers slide between hers that he forgot what he wanted to say. "What's wrong?"

She shook her head and lied to him. "Nothing."

"Elle—" The rumble of an eighteen wheeler stopped him. He needed clothes. The driver would have some, and he didn't know when they'd see somebody else on this lonely road. They could keep talking after he had pants on. He grabbed Elle's other hand. "Stand in the road. Stop the truck."

Her eyes widened in understanding. "He'll have a suitcase." They worked so well together, sharing thoughts almost as easily as words. It had to work out between them.

"Yup."

"We can ask him for clothes."
"Y-Actually, I was thinking we'd steal some."

Chapter Six

Elle looked at her bodyguard in disgust, and not because he literally wasn't human. "We'll what?"

Adam ran a hand over his scruffy, far-too-sexy jaw. "He's not going to give us an outfit." He looked her up and down, making her all too aware of her torn jeans and her jiggling breasts. After everything, she shouldn't want him looking at her with hungry eyes. But she did. His gaze snapped back up to hers, stubborn and strong. "I'm not letting some stranger suggest his price, either." He practically growled the words, his wolf showing through. How had she never seen it before?

She crossed her arms, trying to tame her chest and put up a wall between them. "We don't know the driver's an asshole."

"He's a man. One look at you, and I know exactly what he'll be thinking."

"We don't even know it's a man. Women can drive trucks, too." She picked her way onto the middle of the highway, bare feet cold with every asphalt step, and waved her arms.

Adam stood behind the bike, keeping the handlebars between the stranger and his impressive bits and pieces. "Could be a woman. Could be Mother-fucking-Theresa. But odds are against it. Odds are, it's a man, and he's in the middle of nowhere, been on the road a long time, and if he's flagged down by a woman without a bra with her sweet ass hanging out of her pants, guess what he's going to want."

She narrowed her eyes. *The same way you want me? In bed but not in a lifelong relationship?* "You are such a misanthrope."

"I prefer the term realist."

"The realist werewolf. That's a new one."

The truck slowed, and she felt Adam's eyes on her body. Was he looking at her ass again? She had to stop liking his attention. He was a werewolf. She'd spent their ride out to the middle of nowhere wrapping her brain around Adam the wolf. The time had helped her settle on a few important facts:

One, the wolf wasn't what made Phillip scary. He scared her because he was a violent, possessive asshole. Being a werewolf just made him worse because he was a violent, possessive asshole with fangs and claws.

Two, Adam might be a werewolf, too, but he was still Adam. A year and a half of friendship wasn't suddenly invalidated over something he couldn't help. If anything, she'd be safer because he could fight Phillip on equal terms. Really, it would be great...except for one thing, the terrible thing she'd realized about halfway here.

Three, as Phillip's mate, she knew how werewolf mates worked. His fascination with her had started the moment they'd met. He'd swept her off her feet with exotic dates and obvious signs of affection. When they were together, he couldn't keep his hands off her, holding her hand, touching her leg, putting his palm on the small of her back. It had been flattering, at least until it had gotten scary, but his unequivocal passion for her had been why she'd given him more second chances than any man should have. Adam, on the other hand, hadn't shown any marked romantic interest in her until yesterday, and—also until yesterday—he'd kept his paws completely to himself. She was always the one touching him, not the other way around. Besides, did a woman get more than one werewolf mate? It seemed unlikely.

Four, so the real problem, the one that made her want to cry her eyes out and throw things like a toddler, was that if Adam was a werewolf, he had a mate. And it wasn't her. She would one day lose him to some other woman, one he'd fall for at first sight and shower with affection and put his hands and mouth all over in wonderful ways, and she could do nothing but wait for it to happen.

Put it all together, and she needed to get Adam back to Los Lobos, see if anyone there could fix the Phillip Problem, and leave Adam to his fated future before the stirrings of love she felt turned into something so solid and real her heart would be shattered when he left her. Hell, maybe he had a mate already waiting for him back home. The thought pissed her off, left her scowling in anger right as the truck stopped beside her.

"Need a lift?" The driver, indeed a man, looked from her to Adam, eyes wary as he gazed at the big man. "Why's he nekkid?" He cleared his throat, blushing. "Never mind. I don't want to know."

She forced what she hoped was a reasonably pleasant expression onto her face. Her troubles weren't the trucker's fault, and she needed him in a generous mood before Adam turned felonious. "Actually, that's why we pulled you over. We don't need a lift, but we were hoping we could beg a set of clothes off of you." The man wasn't as broad in the shoulders as Adam and more than a little paunchier in the gut, but a T-shirt and belted jeans would probably work. Now for the hard part. "I don't have any money on me, but if you give me an address, I will be happy to send cash as soon as I'm able. In a few days, tops."

His gaze hooded. Of course he didn't believe her. *I'll put cash in the mail?* It sounded like such a lie, even to her, and she knew she meant it.

She didn't want Adam to rob the guy, but they were on a motorcycle, it was early May in Wyoming, and clothes were not optional. What other options did she have? She looked back at Adam. He stood at full attention behind the motorcycle, and even with no stated plan between them, she knew he waited for her signal or the trucker's motion to spring into action. One nod, and Adam would protect her and take what he needed.

"Those chainy things look an awful lot like that, uh, Tammy jewelry Lady Gaga wore at the Grammys."

She turned back to the trucker, who eyed her earrings in fascination. She touched them. They were, in fact, the prototype for what Gaga had worn. "Thamani. Thah-*mahn*-ee. It means *precious* in Swahili." The media kept mispronouncing her company's name as Tammany, like she'd named it after the defunct American political group instead of a beautiful African word. This did not surprise her. Irritated her. But didn't surprise her.

"Yeah. That." He cleared his throat and quit staring at the gold chain she'd woven into two holes on one side and a different length chain she'd woven into two holes and a cartilage piercing on the other. It wasn't a finished piece, but the thin asymmetry was indicative of her style.

Her irritation over the media's mispronunciation wore off, and she blinked as she realized a man in a mustard-stained Chicago Cubs hoodie had recognized her work. "You follow high-fashion jewelry?"

He laughed, a hand in the air warding off the notion as ridiculous. "Oh, I don't. But my husband is nuts for it. Anything Gaga does, right? Not that I'll ever be able to afford him one of those. How'd you come by it? Even the tiny stuff costs a paycheck." He grimaced. "I looked."

She couldn't help a grin. Score one for Adam; the driver was a man. He was, however, deeply wrong about the driver hitting on her. There might be a way out of this that didn't involve larceny. Would the trucker believe her if she told him she *was* Thamani? In this setting, wearing this lack of an outfit, probably not. Wait, he had a cell phone in the cupholder. "Thamani's owned by Elle Montgomery. Look her up on your phone." Since her star-studded debut, she'd been interviewed for a few human interest pieces— nothing too high profile. But it meant her name and picture, in all its Photoshopped glory, were out there and easy to find.

Giving her a strange look, he did as she requested. He showed her the most popular photo of her, the one where she'd been digitally bleached to nearly as pale as Adam. At least her black hair spiraled around her in its natural bounce. Unlike now with the untamed afro the motorcycle had created.

Maybe he still wouldn't believe her. She sighed. "Photoshop. And it's been a bad-hair day." She patted her frizzy puff. "Bad day in general."

He nodded his head slowly, like she was a crazy person. "Apparently."

"Your husband doesn't have pierced ears, does he?"

"No." He shook the phone at her. "You're saying you're this woman who makes these things?"

"Yeah, I'm Elle. Good to meet you." Still with no idea if he believed her, she picked up her foot and showed off the delicate, gold rope around her ankle with its loose assortment of mismatched beads. It was one of the first pieces she'd been truly proud of, and she never took it off. "I never put this one up for sale. I will give it to you with a signed note of authenticity. I can have the official certificate mailed when I talk to my agent. What I want in return is for my friend over there to get his pick of clothes from your suitcase." She crossed her arms. "I could use a shirt, too."

Once more, the trucker looked at the phone then looked at her, examining the lines of her real face against the mostly real ones on screen. After a moment, he pulled his suitcase into the passenger seat.

Was she really about to trade a seven hundred fifty dollar piece of gold art for clothes out of a trucker's bag?

She glanced back at Adam, keeping vigilant sentry and partial modesty. Was she really in love with a man who was destined for someone else?

Yes. To both those questions, the answer was yes.

***

Mouth dry, heart squeezed tight, Adam turned off the road and into the rocky forest outside Los Lobos. A road didn't pass through town, keeping outsiders out, but you could make it with an off-road vehicle, like his bike. The landscape had shifted drastically in the past hour, from miles of grassy nothing to the evergreen hills and striped gray rocks of his home. They'd passed idyllic pools and fields starting to blossom with spring wildflowers, and every mile beckoned him farther.

Home. He was bringing his mate home.

Elle held him tightly, and he wondered what thoughts kept her so quiet. They hadn't spoken since he'd slid on the ill-fitting outfit—ill-fitting but far better than nothing. He was grateful and humbled by Elle's sacrifice; that anklet meant a lot to her. At least, after he dressed, she'd accepted the offer of his jacket. She'd rested, unmoving against his back, for the majority of the ride.

Now that they were truly here, a place he hadn't seen in ten long years, he wanted nothing more than to push on until they passed the old barn and he was eating a crappy burger at Gee's Bar.

An unlikely dream scenario. In all likelihood, Ryker, the pack's enforcer and the most vicious fighter Adam had ever met, would find them before they got close, kill him, and scare Elle so badly she would run for the Canadian border. He needed to explain the situation to Elle in a way she understood. No, in a way she would believe him regarding the severity.

He stopped his bike by the edge of a wide, shallow stream, cut the motor, and waited for Elle to adjust to the stillness. After a moment she leaned back, and her hands slipped down his abs to rest on his thighs. It felt good, so blissfully right, to be close to her like this with the wind through shivering aspens and the quiet patter of the brook the only sounds. As the fumes of the motorcycle dissipated into the forest, the smell of ponderosa pine and clean water, mulch and new grass soothed him.

Maybe this could work. Ryker wasn't a total ass. Hell, he'd had a blood oath to obey Magnum, and he'd still done a helluva lot better job protecting the pack from Magnum's excesses than Adam. Maybe if he squeezed in an explanation before Ryker killed him, they could work something out for Elle's protection.

Maybe. It all depended on who ruled as alpha. Drew Tao? Because that would be helpful. Or somebody new? Somebody who might be even more deranged than their old alpha?

"What did you stop for?" Elle asked, her voice loud in the forest's stillness.

"This is not going to be a joyful homecoming."

She huffed a disbelieving breath. "Yeah, you've mentioned you were a bad guy." She leaned forward until they were face-to-face. "I know you, Adam. You weren't as bad as you thought."

He shook his head. "I left ten years ago, Elle. I was eighteen and did things I'm not proud of. Hurt members of my pack." He looked away from her disbelieving gaze. "I don't even know who's in charge right now or what things are like. Humans—"

"Aren't supposed to go to Los Lobos. You've mentioned that, too. Look." She touched his chin, turning him back to face her. Her dark eyes filled with compassion. "You were eighteen—a kid. Anyone with a lick of sense will give you a second chance to see what kind of man you've become. And you're a good man." She released his jaw, but he couldn't look away from the faith in her gaze. "I'm not going back to Boulder while Phillip and his pack of hired goons are after me. You told me wolves weren't all like him, and I believe you. Let's go to your people, to your *pack*. Let's talk to them like they're reasonable, uh, werewolves."

She stumbled over the terms, and her sweet fluster drove him to touch her. His fingers twined in her wild hair—she was gonna lose it when she saw the crazy, lovely mess—and he pressed his forehead to hers.

To his surprise, she stiffened and pulled back. He tried to let her go, but his fingers caught in the tangle of her hair. "Oh, uh...." He didn't want to yank his hand out and hurt her.

She laughed, breaking the tension—what was this tension about?—and leaned forward so he could unwind himself. Face down where he couldn't see her expression, she swallowed thickly and said in a nervous voice, "You're not, uh, my mate, right? What we have, it's not...matehood?"

Oh. He grimaced and kept his mouth shut until

his hand was free and she could look up. He wanted to see her face. He wanted to look her in the eyes and tell her the truth, but the fear in her voice…. Phillip had abused the word, turning it into a weapon. She didn't even like the idea of mates because what he saw as natural and beautiful, she saw as forced. It would make what he felt seem less real to her if she thought he didn't choose her of his own free will.

He picked his words carefully. Eventually, he'd tell her the truth, but one problem at a time. First they needed to get into town. "I'm here because I genuinely care about you. You're my best friend." She nodded, her gaze dropping before returning to his. He couldn't decipher her thoughts, so he kept talking, trying to convey what she meant to him without scaring her. "When you found me, I was a depressed alcoholic with no purpose. Since you came into my life, it has color again. Meaning." He touched her cheek, made her look up. Her expression conveyed nothing, her eyes too shaded in the dancing shadows of the trees. He didn't know how she'd take his words, but he spoke them anyway. "My body is alive because my heart beats. My soul is alive because of you."

Tears formed in the corners of her eyes. "Oh, Adam." She cupped her hand around his nape and pulled him to her. They kissed, lips melding, tongues clinging, bodies thrumming and alive, and so full of want. He wrapped his arms around her waist, pressing her close. He wanted to drag her off the bike and take her right here in the woods, on the edge of his homeland. To lay her down on a carpet of pine leaves by the sounds of the brook and beneath the canopy of the trees. To finally claim her as his with the love of their bodies and a mark on the spot where her shoulder curved into her neck.

His mate. His best friend. The love of his life.

She pulled back first, licking the taste of his kiss from her lips. Her tears dropped, spilling in rivulets down her cheeks.

"Why are you crying?" He stroked his thumb across her face, catching the next drop as it fell.

She sniffed, wiped her face on the flannel sleeve of the trucker's wardrobe, and pulled even farther away. "We need to get into town. Let's go before Phillip catches up."

He wanted to protest until she said the asshole's name. Phillip may not know what route they'd taken, but he'd be an idiot not to know where they were going, and Craig and Jim could get him there. Adam must get Elle into the safety of Los Lobos and then hope for the best.

He started the bike, Elle wrapped her arms back around him, and they continued through the spring-thickened forest.

It wasn't long before the first desolate house came into view. He slowed as they passed the Connors' old estate, a once-thriving ranch where they'd held an annual bash at the summer solstice, serving endless mugs of home-brewed beer under strings of colored lights.

The windows had been smashed in, the roof caved in numerous places, and the whole abode abandoned. He shuddered, appalled at the change. Before he'd left, an exodus had already begun, wolves sneaking out in the night to escape Magnum's cruel reign. The Connors, though, were a local light on the outskirts of the pack land, far enough away to make a reasonable escape from the shit going down in the village. If they were gone....

He pushed his bike faster, finding abandoned home after home, each in worse shape than the last, each one another testament to Magnum's atrocities.

Hell, what had become of his pack? What was he bringing Elle back to?

It wasn't long before he noticed a wolf dancing in and out of the trees around them, russet fur a stark contrast with the spring green.

Ryker had found them, and he wanted Adam to know it.

He acknowledged the enforcer with a salute and slowed his bike, but until Ryker stopped them, he'd keep moving toward the safety of town. After another mile, Ryker dashed ahead, his wolf's legs faster on the uneven ground than Adam could be with a precious human on his bike.

So they'd have a "welcoming" committee when they arrived. He only hoped they'd listen before attacking, or he would turn Elle around and plow to the Canadian border himself.

Chapter Seven

Adam's motorcycle slowed as they approached fresh construction at what appeared to be the outskirts of a town. Elle hadn't known what to expect of Los Lobos, but burnt-out shell after wrecked shell of once-good homes hadn't been it. At least the few residences here, in the town itself, seemed in good repair. Fresh paint, new wood, solid construction—these newer buildings were the first things she'd seen without gaping holes. Nearby, what she'd guess was a town hall was going up. A beacon of new hope in a town gone to shit, she might call it.

Speaking of hope, she didn't have much for herself. She'd worked up the guts to flat out ask Adam if they were mates, and he'd said many beautiful words, words she'd long to hear if they were both human. But he hadn't said the one thing that mattered.

She squeezed him anyway, unable to help herself. A line of men came out to meet them, forming a shield between her and Adam and the entrance to the village. The men stood with pride, heads high and figures lean but not gaunt. Los Lobos was a town in the process of righting itself, and it showed in the people.

Uh, the *wolves.*

Adam sighed in what sounded like relief. "Drew Tao." He nodded at the man in the center. "Good to see you here."

"I wish I could say the same, Adam Hunt." The dark-haired man, Drew she supposed, strode forward, a Native American man behind him and to the left, keeping pace. He must be the enforcer, Ryker.

An inauspicious beginning. Elle kept her arm encircling Adam, but poked her head around, trying to get a better view of the situation. "He's here for me," she said. "I'm having a werewolf problem."

Drew and Ryker shared a look, communicating silently in the way of old friends. How she wished she knew what they were thinking.

A man in the back row crossed his arms. "Bringing a human doesn't help his case. Humans aren't welcome here, so I recommend you two turn around and head back where you came from."

Ryker cleared his throat, and the man took a nervous step back.

Drew eyed her carefully. "We make exceptions for mates."

She barely managed to keep a reaction off her face. Adam hadn't mentioned that human mates were allowed in, but he had repeated over and over that she wouldn't be. It felt like a slap. She needed these wolves' help, though. If it took a lie to get Drew Tao to listen to her story, then Adam would have to deal. "Well, good because—"

"Elle is my mate," Adam said, obviously thinking along the same lines. His voice rang out clear and low, with no hesitation in the lie, and it sounded so good. Frustration made her want to scream, but she kept it in. Adam didn't look at her, didn't acknowledge their shared plan with a glance or even a touch, just kept talking to his alpha. "A lot has changed in ten years—with this town. It's astonishing. A lot has changed with me as well. All I'm asking for is a chance. Hear Elle out."

Drew once again flicked a look to Ryker, this time with a slow mile. "Is your chance for her or for you?"

Elle bristled. She didn't know exactly what had happened before, but a decade had passed. A town this in need of a makeover should accept all the willing hands it could get.

But, instead of protesting, Adam said, "Her."

She put a hand on her hip. "We're a package deal. You don't want my money to help bring this place back to scratch—because it could clearly use it— or his hands to do some labor, we'll find some other pack that will appreciate an honest contribution."

To her surprise, her words sent a chuckle through their ranks. Drew took another step toward them, eyes bright, almost amber as the wolf shone through. "You don't seem very afraid, little human."

Adam stiffened, putting more of himself between her and the pack alpha as his hand reached back to rest protectively on her thigh. He might still be her bodyguard, but she was sick of being afraid. If this jerkoff alpha wanted to play tough wolf, she could handle it. She'd seen a raging werewolf, and Drew wasn't it. Let him try to intimidate her, to see if she'd fold. She swung off the bike, standing up to her full height. Adam nearly kicked the motorcycle over scrambling up beside her, but she wouldn't let him make a wall between her and the alpha.

She did let Adam take her hand. They interlocked fingers, drawing strength from each other in the connection. "Adam seems to think you're one of the good guys, not some psychopath like the last werewolf I met. If you're what he says you are—a leader he can look up to—then you'll be fair enough to at least hear us out. Adam was eighteen when he left. I don't know what he did before then, but judging from what's left behind, something much worse came after him. He left because he wanted to be a good person." She wrinkled her nose. "Good wolf." Eventually, she'd get used to saying it. She cocked her head and issued her last taunt. If this didn't work, they needed to hop back on the bike and go. Quickly. "If you can't see him for the good man he is, then I don't think you're smart enough to help me anyway."

One of the wolves behind Drew growled a threat, stepping forward. Ryker scowled, as though offended on behalf of his alpha. Adam's hand tightened on hers, drawing her back.

Drew, though, just laughed, louder this time. His stance and voice were full of confidence as he stepped to the side, giving them a path into town. "Proceed straight to Gee's and check in. We'll talk after you've had a chance to eat and"—he looked them up and down, no doubt taking in their equally bedraggled states—"freshen up." His steady gaze turned to Adam. "I assume you remember the way?"

Adam nodded, slid back onto the motorcycle,

and motioned for Elle to do the same. Before he started the motor, he spoke. "We've had a tail since Boulder. Packless mongrel named Phillip." Elle slid her arms back around Adam at Phillip's name. She could fake bravado with this crew, but not about him. He still terrified her. "He's gathered a couple of Magnum's men, Craig and Jim. I assume, even without our scent to follow, they'll lead him here. I'd guess within the next few hours."

Drew's eyes flashed darkly, and Ryker's fists clenched as he rolled back and forth on his feet, ready for action. Drew nodded and lifted an eyebrow at her. "I take it this is the wolf problem you were referring to?"

She nodded. "Phillip thinks he's my mate. But he's not. Adam is." Oh, how she wished those words were true.

***

Adam had called her his mate, and she hadn't freaked out. What did that mean? Was she okay with the idea? Did she realize he'd meant it, or did she think he'd lied to get her into town? It felt so good to speak the truth out loud. He paced their room trying to sort out what to do next, Oshun hissing at him from under the bed every time he got too close. Of course, Gee, who'd grunted and handed them a key and said nothing, had put mates in the same room. This one with only one bed.

What a relief the new alpha had made it legal to bring mates into the city. His faith in Drew Tao, so far anyway, didn't seem misplaced. It would be good to work for an alpha who thought of the good of the pack and not merely his own twisted desires. Now Adam needed to prove to Drew and Ryker that he wasn't the same asshole who'd left and that he would be a productive member of the pack if they let him stay. Then he needed to prove to Elle that she'd love being mates with him and convince her to stick by him, bear his children, and live happily ever after in werewolf country. Not much to ask, right?

The shower kicked on, and Elle started humming a sexy R&B number. She was a shower singer with a gravelly voice that made him want to press her into the tiles and lick the water off her skin. It took him a moment to realize he'd quit pacing to stand and stare at the bathroom door.

Did he think he needed to convince Drew to let him stay and *then* convince Elle to be his mate in truth? He had it backwards. He needed Elle now. If she was with him, nothing else mattered much. Hell, he'd live on the moon if that's where she'd share his bed. Before he could think about it too much, he knocked on the bathroom door. "Elle? Tell me now if you don't want me coming in." No answer. Could she hear him over the water? "Elle?" He put his hand on the doorknob and his forehead against the wood.

Her low laughter dripped of sexual need. Or maybe that was his randy imagination? "I thought you'd made it pretty clear what would happen if I didn't say anything. I'm waiting...."

He couldn't get the door open or his clothes off fast enough.

It was a terrible idea to let Adam in. She knew exactly what he wanted—because she wanted it so badly herself. Making love to Adam now would only make the end harder, but she couldn't help herself. One excellent night, and then they'd solve the Phillip problem and she'd leave him to his pack and his future, whatever it may be.

The thought of life without Adam made her chest hurt.

Then he slipped inside the sliding glass door, and she forgot all about tomorrow. Steam circled their bodies as he pushed her up against the wall. His hard body pressed into hers, his erection already stiff and so thick. One arm encircled her waist, lifting her up. The other wove into her hair, holding her in place. Exhilaration sent her blood racing and her heart pounding, heating her up, making her burn.

With lust-drunk eyes he looked her over, his gaze caressing her face, searching her. He didn't take possession like she expected, holding back as she squirmed against him, trying to drive them forward into the bliss she wanted with him. Only with him. "What are you waiting for?"

"I've wanted you for so long," he said, voice guttural with need. "I want to make sure this is what you want, too, because I'm tired of waiting. I want you, all of you. Now."

She hoped the water hid her threatening tears. She'd been afraid of things changing between them, but now that he was back home, change would happen whether she wanted it or not. She needed to give him everything now—her body and her love— because she wanted all of him, too, no matter what the future held. She slid her knee up his water-slick thigh until her leg caught around his hip, opening her body to his. He smelled of leather and grit with a hint of the pine-wood scent that seemed a part of him. She pressed her hand to his heart and found it racing as fast as her own. "I want you, too, joined as lovers the way we've been joined as friends." She met his gaze. "I've wanted you for a long time, but I've been afraid. We're good together, you and I. What we've had? I didn't want to lose it."

His thumb stroked her cheek, his finger quivering with desire even as he held himself back. "We're not losing anything, sweetheart. We're just getting better. I promise." He kissed her.

The erotic press of his wet, naked body created a stark contrast to the sweet promise of his mouth. If his body said dark passion, his lips said kindness. Maybe even love. She gave in, allowing herself this one time to believe—or at least to pretend. "I want to love you slowly, Adam. I want to draw it out. Make it last."

He moaned against her, pressing harder, hips shifting eagerly. His cock, thick and ready, pressed eagerly against her. But all he said was, "You're the boss." His hand spread wide over her back, caressing her in a slow motion that sent shivers up her spine.

If he really had been waiting for "so long" as he said, the poor man was going to have a hard time of it—pun intended. She gave him a teasing grin. "I find myself in your debt, though."

His brows drew together like he didn't understand her reference to this morning's non-mutual satisfaction.

"Think you're up for more than one round?"

He laughed like she'd asked a silly question.

"Good." She dropped to her knees. His laughter stopped abruptly as she took hold of his shaft and pumped once. Twice. "Brace yourself, wolf. I'm good at this."

"Oh, fuck—" She sucked him in, and he put his hands against the wall, catching himself before he toppled. "Oh, fuck, Elle." His breath heaved out in a rush. "That's...oh. Yes."

She cupped his balls in her hands and took him deep with her mouth. His head fell back as he articulated noises that couldn't qualify as words, totally at her mercy.

Blow jobs were fun, taking a man in hand—and mouth—and watching him react, knowing he would do anything to keep it going. But with Adam it felt different—special. She wanted to know him, what he liked, what he reacted to. What spots made him come apart the hardest. She wanted to remember how he felt, every piece of him. The steel of his sex sheathed in soft, wet skin. The way the muscles of his thighs clenched as she changed the pressure and released as she pulled away.

The way he said her name, the only thing he could pronounce with any clarity, with awe in his tone. His hand touched her scalp, his fingers trembling as he stroked her hair.

"I'm...I'm...oh, Elle!" He came, fingers clenching in her hair without holding her against him, giving her the freedom to choose. She held on, sucking the last drop from him. He dropped to his knees, panting in front of her as she swallowed and smiled.

"Debt paid," she whispered. Anxiety took her by surprise. Would he change, replacing her trusted companion with someone new and less kind? Even as the thought crossed her mind, she knew it was Phillip she feared, not the man in front of her. Still, the voices in her head insisted everything would be different now. She'd lost what they had.

Adam huffed a laugh and kissed her mouth then her cheek and her forehead. His arms wrapped around her head, pulling her into his chest in a hold both playful and grateful, every bit the friend she loved. Except they were naked in the shower.

Her fear evaporated with his joy. This was a relationship she could get used to—steady, friendly, lovable Adam, but with X-rated bonus content.

He pulled her into his lap, a sure sign he was feeling protective. Without a word, he got the shampoo bottle, squirted far too much into his hand, and massaged it into her hair.

She closed her eyes and let him take care of her. His hands stayed gentle as his touch grew more sure and steady. After her hair, he got the soap and cleaned them both, running sudsy palms reverently over every part of her. Finally, when they were both cleaned and rinsed, he spoke, his voice like gravel. "One slow, drawn out, lasting love, coming your way as ordered, boss."

She shivered at the promise in his voice. Tomorrow she'd worry about the future. Right now, she wanted Adam's hands on her body and his dick inside   her.

Chapter Eight

Adam dried off his mate and carried her to the bed, every step filled with hope. After he had longed for her for months, Elle finally wanted him. Everything else would work itself out. He laid her down on the bed, and she smiled at him, her eyes bright with anticipation. He took a long look at her naked skin, still dewy from the shower, and debated where to start. *Mine. All mine.* At least for now. Tomorrow he'd work on tomorrow. And every day after, he'd keep working so she never wanted anyone else. She'd given him a chance, and he'd show her exactly why she wanted to be his mate.

He started with a kiss. Her lips moved rhythmically against his as her body arched into him. The urge to take her simmered beneath his too-hot skin, but he tempered his desire with the tender need for closeness. She wanted slow. His mate would have slow. He stroked her body, letting his hands wander at will. When she shivered, he noted it and made sure to return there so she would shiver again and again.

Her tongue slid into his mouth, and the kiss grew deeper. Her hands moved from their secure place on his back to explore him, too. She pressed her fingers into the muscles of his ass, caressed the lines of his hip, slid her fingertips over his arms, as if she, too, would memorize his body. The connection drove him wild, turned the world into a cocoon of her and him and the power of touch.

Her breath hitched, growing faster and deeper. He trailed kisses where his hands had explored. She'd loved his touch on the curve of her waist. He swirled his tongue over the spot and she moaned. Ran his teeth across it and her cries grew louder. Every sound she made spiked his need for her, made him long more to bury himself inside her, to claim her as his own.

Not yet, not yet.

He tasted more of her skin, covered every inch of her with kisses until she squirmed and arched beneath his touch, her body out of her control and into his. When she growled his name, he pressed his mouth to her slick core. She was wet, so wet and ready for him to take her. *Not yet.* He teased her with his tongue, and her hips rose, opening herself to him. "Adam, oh God, Adam, please. Please take me, please."

Her voice was as intoxicating as her sweet taste. He took her with his tongue, crazed with need for her, and she lurched upward again. He held her hips down, forcing her still for him.

She screamed again, fingers digging into his scalp. "Oh, God, your cock, Adam. I need your cock inside me. Right now. I want to come with you inside me."

Yes, boss. He didn't know if he said it or just thought it, but he scrambled up and put his hands on either side of her face as he kissed her mouth. Her legs wrapped around him, and he fit their bodies together. A thrust and he was home. She arched her back, bringing him deeper inside. She came, her walls squeezing around him as he pushed in and out, the slick friction driving him to the edge of his control.

Her whole body shuddered as the waves of her orgasm spread from her core to her extremities. He'd done that. He'd treated her right.

As her climax subsided, she didn't stop moving. Her hips bucked harder, from sweet touch to frenzied need. He cupped her breast and teased her nipple, kissed her neck, ran his teeth over the sensitive skin. She wanted to come again, and he would get her there.

She pushed his shoulder, and he flipped them over so she could ride him. Her hips ground down onto his, and he gasped at the sensation. His hips rose in time with hers, meeting her thrust for thrust. Her chin tilted to the sky with abandon as she murmured in the nonsense of a perfect fuck. Her fingertips dug into his chest as she rose a last time and dropped down hard with a cry. "Oh God. Oh, God. Adam. Adam." She collapsed onto his chest. "I love you."

He froze, every muscle locking up at that word, every selfish instinct to take, have, possess gone slack with the need to share, connect, be one. He turned them to the side where he could hold her. Instinct overrode every thought, and he bit down on her shoulder, connecting them as tightly as he could as his orgasm took him and his mind reeled into ecstasy.

She whimpered, her shaking fingers taking slow tours of his back as he clutched her against him. "I love you, too, Elle. God, I love you so much."

He could barely move, he trembled so badly, but somehow, with her help, he got her tucked up against him under the sheets, their bodies slack and so beautifully spent.

"That was so fucking awesome," she gasped out.

He laughed, and the words were at the tip of his tongue to say, *See, being mates isn't so bad*. It seemed like the right time—better than any other, anyway—to make it clear what she meant to him. Her gaze turned up to his, satisfied as a woman could get. He kissed her forehead then her nose then her mouth.

Her smile curled up, so pleased. She kissed the center of his chest, put her hand there, and curled up against him. "Do you really?"

"Hm?" he asked.

"Love me?"

He tightened his arms around her. "Oh, yeah. I have for a long time. I've wanted you since the moment I first saw you." He laughed, a little self-consciously. "Actually, since the moment I smelled you. You smell good. At the fire when we met, I took my face shield off, and *boom*. It was you. Only you."

She laughed. "Silly wolf. Smell is not a reason to love someone."

There it showed again, her worry that mate-dom interfered with love. He needed to convince her otherwise. "True, but I said I *wanted* you then. I fell in *love* with you over this year and a half, watching you relentlessly chase your dream. Watching your passion for art and your savvy for business. Watching you celebrate success and persevere after every setback. I fell in love with you eating pho and watching television. Laughing over celebrity gossip. Enjoying the sight of you dancing around the house in those work pants with the ever-expanding hole and wishing I could stick my hand up it."

That made her laugh.

He took a deep breath. Now was the perfect time to tell her. She would take it well, and they'd figure out what to do with their lives together. He licked his lips. "See, Elle, being—"

Pounding at the door stopped his words. She lifted herself off him, alerted by the insistence of the noise.

"All hands on deck," Drew yelled through the door. "You wanted to prove yourself, Hunt. Here's your shot."

Elle looked at him, eyes wide with fear. She quickly gathered clothing.

Out the window, smoke blew past their open glass. He took a big breath, smelling the air.

Fire. Phillip and his crew had started a fire.

He launched up and tossed on his clothes. Elle was buttoning up the ridiculously large top from the trucker's bag. He grabbed her hand and tugged her with him. "A building's burning. I have to help."

She nodded. "Of course." The quiver in her tone, though, told him how afraid she was.

He couldn't take her into a fire. He also couldn't leave her alone, not with Phillip and his men on the loose. So what did he do?

Hand in hand, they raced down the stairs. The bar had emptied out. Gee, an enormous bear of a man—literally. He was a werebear—stood outside his door, surveying the chaos as people ran away from or toward the fire, depending on how sane they were.

Adam wasn't one of the sane ones. The fire called him forward, challenging him to conquer it. "Where's the truck?" he asked.

"We don't have one," Gee answered, scowling. "No fire department."

"What?" Adam asked, appalled. "How do you not have a fire department?" The question was rhetorical. It didn't matter. What did matter was getting someone down there who knew what they were doing. He took Elle's hand and placed it in Gee's. "You've got a fire department now. Watch her. Please." He touched Elle's chin, forcing her scared eyes up to his. "She's my life."

She closed her eyes, scared but trusting him. "Go. Help."

He kissed her forehead. "Stay with Gee. No one will hurt you. Okay?"

Gee snorted. "Get your fuzzy wolf ass to the fire and do something useful. I'll watch your mate."

Adam didn't want to leave Elle, but he needed to go help.

"Go," she whispered. "You saved me from fire. Save somebody else."

Adam ran toward the fire, and Elle watched him go, a lump in her throat and a pain in her heart. It was completely irrational, but he'd found her at a fire. What if he found his true mate at this fire? Tonight had been epic, the definition of a soul connection—or so she'd have said. Her body ached in ways she'd never felt. Her soul felt at peace like she'd never known.

She wanted to be close to him, as close as she

could safely get. "Can we walk that way?"

"Toward the fire?" Gee asked.

"No," she said. "Toward Adam." She wanted Adam, loved him. Damn the whole mate-bonding thing, Elle did not roll over and play dead. If she wanted something, she fought for it. Fuck destiny. What she and Adam shared was worth fighting for.

Gee took a too-slow pace toward the blaze, but she wasn't stupid enough to race ahead of her protection. If Phillip had set the fire as a distraction, he'd be looking for her. She wouldn't make it easy for him by leaving her escort. As they got closer, the sounds of yelling and the smell of smoke pervaded her senses. She'd avoided fire ever since the apartment, not even lighting her fireplace in the depth of winter. But Adam would be there, risking himself for the safety of a town that had sent him into an alcoholic spiral. She wanted to be near him, even help if she could. She definitely needed to be with him afterward to make sure the conjunction of the town and the fire didn't trigger a relapse into a bottle. They were a team.

After a block of silence, Gee rumbled, "Somebody wanted a clear declaration."

She frowned, unsure what he meant or even how she felt about the behemoth man. The first time they'd met, while Adam got them a key, he'd been taciturn and eyed them with suspicion. "I've known Adam for a while now. He's a good man. This town would do well to give him a second chance."

Gee laughed, a low bellow. "I meant Adam wanted a clear declaration of you. His mark's directly on top of an old one."

"Mark...?" Adam had bitten her sometime during

their colossal round of sex. She hastily yanked the too-big shirt back over her collarbone. It kept slipping. Then his words sank in. "What do you mean *old one*?"

"Mate mark. Somebody claimed you before. Adam lined his bite up to cover it, ensuring the whole town knows he doesn't share."

Emotions crashed one after another, wild as the fire in front of them. Phillip had marked her? How horrifying. He had no right. Then Adam had covered it up with his own mark. He had no right to do so, either, but she couldn't find it in herself to be angry, not after what they'd shared. Hell, she wanted to mark him back, claim him equally.

She touched her neck over the place he'd bitten. "I'm not his…. Wait, you can have two mates?"

Gee shrugged. "It's rare but possible."

Her heart pounded. "So I could be Adam's mate even if I'm Phillip's?"

The bear's eyebrows shot up. "You *are* Adam's mate. Isn't that what you told us when you came here? It's why we let you into town."

Realizing her mistake, she shut her lips. Then she smiled. Adam had told her he'd wanted her since he first smelled her. Weird as that sounded, it indicated desire at first sight. He'd guarded her faithfully from the moment they'd met, even arguing with her every time she told him to take a night off. And yeah, he wasn't a pushy asshole like Phillip, trying to force himself on her at every opportunity…but Adam wasn't a pushy asshole. He was a good man who respected her wishes. A man who would never leave her for another woman or stray for even a single night.

She was Adam's mate. Joy made her steps light even as they approached the chaos Phillip had wrought. Let him do his worst. She and Adam would take him down. Together.

They reached a corner of gawkers staring up at a two-story home. Fire consumed the back wall, sending black smoke and a tornado of sparks into the evening. Elle caught her breath at the beauty of the flame and the horrible smell of destruction. A perimeter had been erected around the block, enforced by a few young people. A group of capable-looking men and women gathered around Adam, listening as he issued orders. He looked fierce, guiding the fight against the fire. Her heart skipped at the vision he made. Her man. Her mate.

"Well?" Gee asked, bringing her back to the present. "Are you or are you not?"

She threw back her shoulders and grinned. "Fated and mated, baby."

The expression Gee gave her was a little too smug for her liking. She had the eeriest sensation he'd guided her to the realization.

She narrowed her eyes at him. "You tossing wise old man crap my way?"

His eyes shone with mirth though he never smiled. "I have no idea what you're talking about."

"I bet you don't," she muttered. Adam headed into the burning house, and she forgot all about Gee or anyone else. What the hell was her man doing going *into* a burning house? They didn't even have fireman's clothes!

"Woah, slow yourself." Gee clapped an arm on her shoulder. She hadn't even realized she'd gone toward the building. Gee's hand became a clamp.

"Get down!"

The roar of trucks blasted through the night. She landed face down in the dirt—when a werebear moved a person, the person *moved*.

"Look out!" Gee roared, yanking children out of the way as two trucks swerved through the crowd.

Two of the goons from the hotel hung out of the windows of one truck, whooping like idiots at a backwoods fair. A wolf from the crowd leaped at them, grabbed one of the men, and dragged him through the window. A fight broke out as pack members piled onto the truck, half human, half animal, like they'd tear the men apart. Cries of "Magnum's boys!" rent the air in a frenzy of hatred.

Elle backpedaled away as terror sent every nerve on alert. She had to get out of there.

Gunfire erupted. She screamed at the repeated pops, turned, and ran.

The other truck cut her off. The door opened, and Phillip's filthy hands grabbed onto her. "Hello, mate."

She brought a knee up and rammed it between his legs. He groaned and bent over, releasing her just enough that she could get away.

Panicked, she ran.

"Bitch!" he yelled. His footsteps slammed onto the pavement and pounded behind her.

Phillip was coming for her.

Chapter Nine

The house still smoldered where the fire had started, but the main of it was under control. The blaze would've been easy to handle with a trained crew and a few basic supplies, but Los Lobos's fire plan was only slightly better than "lots of buckets." Even if he and Elle didn't stay, he'd talk to Drew about organizing a volunteer crew and maybe even come back to train them, if the alpha let him. Arson wasn't the only way a fire started, and he wanted his pack to be better prepared.

He exited the building with the roar of the fire still in his ears and the heat still stinging his skin in red reminders that neither man nor wolf was meant to run through fire.

He loved it.

Outside, the chaos reigned even harsher than the blaze had been. A truck had been overturned, and two wolves—Jim and Craig by the looks of them—had been literally torn to pieces. Apparently, the pack was keen to be rid of any trace of the old alpha. Adam didn't blame them. Another truck rocked back and forth as townsmen tipped it over.

Where was Elle in this mess? Fear curled through him, and he scented the air. Between fire and all the bodies, he couldn't smell her. "Elle!" Where was that fucking werebear? He turned.

Gee was nearly on top of him.

"Fuck! Where did you come from?" How did he not smell a damn bear? "Where's Elle?"

Gee pointed toward the forest. "Phillip has her."

Rage made his vision go red. "What? But you were supposed to—hell." *Yell later. Protect Elle now.* Panicked, his wolf took over, and he charged into the woods on all fours.

Before he could see them, he smelled their scent—just the two of them—and heard their angry progress through the forest. The smell of metal and gasoline warned him Phillip had transportation nearby.

"You'll learn respect, little mate," Phillip said. "I wanted to do this nicely, but you wouldn't listen."

"I'm not your mate," Elle spat back. "I have a mate. His name is Adam Hunt, and you are nothing compared to him."

Adam nearly tripped at the sound of his name. She'd called him her mate. His heart soared.

"I'm your mate," Phillip snarled. The smack of an open hand on flesh echoed in the trees, like Phillip had slapped her. That coward was so fucking dead.

"I'm going to get away from your ass," Elle said, voice dangerously low. "And then Adam's going to kill you."

Damn right. His mate needed him. He howled, forced an extra burst of speed, and hit a clearing as Phillip pulled a bike to standing.

Elle saw him. Fear lit her eyes as she stiffened.

Then she sighed in recognition. She knew him, even in wolf form. Of course she did. They were meant to be.

Phillip grabbed her around the waist, trying to haul her onto his motorcycle. In a move Adam had taught her, she jammed an elbow back into his stomach and snapped her head back, ramming her skull into Phillip's nose. Blood shot out of his nostrils as the cartilage shattered. He screamed in pain and released her.

Elle ran straight for Adam. "I hope you're Adam."

He barked a hello, passed her, and pounced. Phillip went down. The man spun, faster than Adam had anticipated, as he morphed from man to beast.

"I made him a promise, Adam. I'm guessing you heard it," Elle yelled, her tone full of steel. "I got away from him. Your turn."

He snarled in acknowledgment. Nobody hurt his woman. Nobody made her afraid. Nobody owned her. Phillip had broken everything wolves held holy about mates.

Phillip growled and faced him, teeth drawn back in fear and anger. He lunged, trying for a killing blow.

Adam sidestepped him, took him by the ruff, and shook. A crack signaled Phillip's neck had broken. With a final rush of air, Phillip went limp. Adam dropped his kill and kicked dirt onto the asshole.

Breathing heavily, he turned back to Elle. She'd said to kill him. Now, how would she feel about it?

She took a few steps into the clearing. "Is he...?"

Adam nodded and started to shift back. She'd looked absolutely terrified when he'd shown up in wolf form. He didn't want to scare her.

"Wait. Be a wolf."

He stopped, letting his wolf come back.

"You can still, uh, think like this, right?" Her breath came in short, fearful bursts. "Do I have to worry about setting off instinct or anything? Don't look you in the eyes or whatever?"

He padded a few steps forward and whined as he shook his head, trying to convey that he remained in control, even if he couldn't do convenient things like talk.

She nodded, somehow understanding anyway. "I need to get used to you like this." She licked her lips nervously then looked askance at her ex-boyfriend, dead beside his motorcycle. The man had set fire to a house and sacrificed four wolves so he could kidnap Elle. The selfish audacity was astounding.

Adam trotted away from him and toward his mate. He wanted to get her out of here and back toward the town. Maybe via a route which didn't take her through the remains of Jim and Craig. He slowed as he got to her, trying to appear as friendly as possible.

Her fingers curled as she eyed him speculatively. He bumped her leg in friendly greeting then looked up at her, waiting for her move. Slowly, she stuck a hand in the fur of his ruff and gripped it between her knuckles. "I'm a cat person, you know. This is love."

He opened his mouth and panted, the closest sound to a laugh he could make. At her nod, he continued forward, leading them home.

Elle had her hands in wolf fur. Adam's wolf fur. He was giant, coming up to her waist, with bright eyes and gorgeous, thick fur the golden blond of his hair.

Had she thought Phillip's fur wiry? Adam's felt as soft as the scruff of the two-day beard he typically sported. Tentatively, she stroked his head. He bumped into her again, and she nearly lost her footing. He made a huffing animal sound of amusement as he stopped and helped her right herself. "Yeah, yeah. Laugh it up, fuzzball."

More playful huffing as they continued forward. By the time they reached the town, the violence was over, the town celebrating victory and the saved house. Gee waved as he saw them return, and Elle returned the gesture. Adam growled, lips pulling back from fangs in a threat. Her instinct said to back away from an angry animal. If it had been Phillip, she would've found the nearest exit point and run.

But it wasn't Phillip. It was Adam. She had a choice to make right now—to run in fear and keep running or to trust Adam and act like herself around the wolf, the same way she did around the man. Swallowing her nerves, she tapped him on the head in a mock reprimand. "Hush, now. He was saving children. Give the bear a break."

Adam stepped between her and Gee, knocking into her with that big, fuzzy body of his as he snarled at the bear. He couldn't say, "Mine! Back off!" any more loudly with words. She supposed the next step would be pissing a circle around her. She didn't feel threatened in the least, though. He was guarding her, not caging her.

She ignored the show of machismo. He couldn't speak in wolf form, so she'd have to speak for him. "That's right. Kiss and make up with Gee." It was not even close to what he'd meant.

He barked in protest and nosed her thigh with his cold muzzle.

"What's that?" This game had potential. She could fill in his speech with whatever she wanted. "You recommend I buy us that house at the edge of town and build a big studio? What a fantastic idea!"

Adam's butt plopped down, and he stared up at her, head cocked, like he didn't think she was serious. His eyes were blue, even as a wolf. Weird. And cool.

"You are moving in, right? Because I'm not living in a town full of wolves unless I've got one in my bedroom."

His tail thumped twice, and she'd swear he smiled.

Drew, the pack alpha, approached them next. "Congratulations, Hunt, and welcome back to Los Lobos. I'm expecting recommendations for your fire crew on my desk in the morning." He glanced from the wolf to Elle and back, a smile slowly growing. "Maybe in a couple of days." He nodded at Elle. "Good to meet you."

"You, too." She gave him a casual two-fingered salute as he jogged off toward a pretty redhead.

Adam licked her hand with his warm tongue then nuzzled her waist, each gesture a show of canine affection.

"This is going to take some getting used to, you know. My boyfriend the dog."

He barked and head butted her in the stomach, hard enough to be playful but not hard enough to hurt.

She laughed and scratched him behind the ear. "Fine. Wolf."

Epilogue

Elle had the warmth of Adam's thick fur at her back and a well-contained fire at her front as she drank hot chocolate and read a book. They'd rebuilt the house at the edge of Los Lobos into a gorgeous, working ranch with a full metal studio. Tonight they'd thrown a party to celebrate moving in, and the whole village had shown up for her and for Adam, their beloved fire chief. She'd been pleasantly surprised by the number of humans in the town, although the wolves weren't so different from people after all. She'd found Los Lobos to be a welcoming community, as beautiful as Colorado in its own way. With a whole pack protecting each other, she would never have to be afraid again.

Adam sighed his wolfie sigh. They'd started doing this in the cold evenings, him lazing around and her curled up against his lean wolf's belly, his fur surrounding her and keeping her warm. But, today, nervous energy consumed her. They'd been living together for a while now, and while Adam seemed content, she wanted something more. "Hey, Wolf?"

He flapped his tail once, signaling his attention. "Do wolves get married?"

She waited for the motion of his tail, one slap for yes, a drag for no. Instead, she nearly toppled backward as he shifted, sliding from wolf to man with amazing speed. He started talking before his vocal chords had fully changed, the sound transitioning from a growl to his human voice as he spoke. "Some do. Some rely on the mate bond. It's forever—way more secure than a modern marriage is." His arms came around her, and he pulled her back against his naked chest. "Why? Want to get married? Name the day." He winked. "I'm there."

She bopped him on the head with her e-reader. "That was the worst proposal ever."

"That wasn't a proposal!" He laughed and kissed her on the cheek. "I can do better. Want a crowd to witness or a private retreat or something sweet or funny or...? Name your scenario, boss. I'll get it done right."

It was her turn to laugh. He still called her "boss" even though she wasn't paying him any more. She'd pointed it out a while ago. He'd winked and said she could still boss him around all she wanted...provided she was naked. Now it was their little joke. She turned in his arms until she knelt in front of him, his naked legs on either side of her and his hands on her shoulders. Naked Adam was distracting, and she needed to concentrate. "I think a good proposal might be in our house, right after we moved in, the remains of our homecoming still decorating the place."

His brow lifted. "You mean tonight." He rubbed her shoulders, his expression turning worried. "I'm sorry. I don't have a plan. I'll come up with something, though...."

Her heart squeezed with nerves as she pulled a black pouch from her pocket and held it out to him.

"What's this?" He emptied the pouch into his palm. Two rings fell out, one shaped for a man and another for a woman, both delicate and hammered with pink-and-green accents in the style of the Black Hills goldsmiths.

She swallowed. "I've been working on new designs based on coloring gold like they do here, copper for pink and silver for the green. I'm releasing a new line this spring. But I figured I needed to practice first. So I made a couple of rings...."

He slid the ring she'd made for him onto his finger. The twisted colors looked good against his skin. "It's incredible." His gaze met hers. "Are you asking me to marry you?"

She crossed her arms. "Well, we are mates, so it shouldn't be a big deal. I want a ceremony I can invite my mother to. I want a dress and...." He smiled at her bluster. She groaned. "How do men do this? I'm totally botching it up. I had a speech. I didn't say any of it." She mock scowled at his cock, standing at attention in front of her. That was the problem with lying against a wolf. The animal changed into a naked man, and the naked man had a naked penis, and then all she could think about were all the fun things she could be doing with that penis. She theorized Adam used his soft, warm, wolfie self as a never-fail tool of seduction. "I blame your dick. I still find it terribly distracting."

"Excellent." He stood up, pulled her with him, and slipped the other ring onto her finger. "Yes. I would be proud to marry you."

"Well, good. Because I made wedding bands to go with these. The set is on point."

He pressed his naked body against her fully clothed one, swaying in time to the rhythm of their heartbeats.

After a moment, she relaxed, reveling in the steady feel of her man, her mate, her fiancé, the wolf she loved. "Take me to bed, wolf."

He stroked her back and kissed her forehead, each touch full of love. "Any time, boss. I'm all yours."

About the Author

Jax Garren is the author of hot, urban paranormal romance like the Austin Immortals and the Tales of the Underlight. Though descended from Valkyries and Vikings (she's part Swedish), Jax was raised a small town girl in the Texas Hill Country. She graduated from The University of Texas with a degree in English and a minor in Latin then found her own Happily Ever After with a handsome engineer who is saving the world through clean energy technology.

Jax can be found at jaxgarren.com, at facebook.com/JaxGarren or on Twitter as @JCGarren. She loves meeting new people, so online or in person, make sure to give her a Viking "Hail!" adventure, and love.